10 : 01

by
lance olsen

D1519986

chiasmus press
PORTLAND

Chiasmus Press

www.chiasmuspress.com
press@chiasmusmedia.net

PRODUCED AND PRINTED IN THE UNITED STATES OF AMERICA
ISBN: 0-9703212-6-0

cover design: Lidia Yuknavitch
layout design: Matthew Warren
cover photo: Mia De Bono
author photo: Andi Olsen

Also by Lance Olsen

NOVELS
Live from Earth
Tonguing the Zeitgeist
Burnt
Time Famine
Freaknest
Girl Imagined by Chance

SHORT STORIES
My Dates with Franz
Scherzi, I Believe
Sewing Shut My Eyes
Hideous Beauties

NONFICTION
Ellipse of Uncertainty
Circus of the Mind in Motion
William Gibson
Lolita: A Janus Text
Rebel Yell: A Short Guide to Writing Fiction

For Andi: 24 : 07 : 365

Note

The complementary hypermedia version of this novel exists at:
www.cafezeitgeist.com/1001.html

You must habit yourself to the dazzle of the light.
-Walt Whitman, *Leaves of Grass*

00 : 00 : 00 : 00

MIDAFTERNOON IN A MOVIE THEATER in the Mall of America. Glary lights before the show make everything seem stark and unfinished to Kate Frazey, a bony aerobics instructor relieving herself of her shocking-pink ski jacket, bunching it on the folded-up seat beside her, and sitting in row three, seat nine, seeing herself as she does so as if from a crane shot among these other filmgoers filtering in and settling down around her. Kate, blond hair so dark it is almost the color of high-fiber breakfast cereal, is Franz Kafka's great-great granddaughter, although she carries no awareness of this within her. She doesn't know her great-great grandfather once had an affair with another bony woman, Grete Bloch, friend of Felice Bauer, to whom Kafka was briefly engaged. Kate doesn't know Grete had a son about whom Kafka never learned, nor that his son was supposed to have died while a child, but was adopted by a Jewish businessman and his wife, and brought to New York in the thirties. Whenever Kate dreams, it is about the plots of Kafka's work, which she has never read because she believes there are already too many stories in the world. Kate dreams that two strangers in top hats and frock coats are always knocking at her door, wanting in. That she

1

is a ninety-pound weight-loss artist dissolving in a cage full of hay in the town square in Prague. That she is a muscular hare darting through a wet field at night and that, no matter how fast she runs, no matter which direction she chooses, the beautiful hounds sleeping within the castle miles away will awaken the next day and chase her down. This is why Kate doesn't sleep unless she has to. This is why she hasn't slept for two nights, why she leans forward now, elbows on knees, concentrating very hard on keeping her glistery brown eyes wide open.

THREE ROWS BACK sits Stuart Navidson, plumping gynecologist with a small practice in Minneapolis. Heart a hummingbird, Stuart hunches over his Palm, reading email, oblivious of the factoids flipping up on the movie screen in front of him. He doesn't care that in a *zip pan* the camera moves so quickly the image in between the original subject and its successor is blurred, nor that the first film fan magazines appeared in 1912. Monday afternoon at the office, he received an email with no subject heading and fake sender address. *Eat shit and die*, it said. Spam, Stuart thought. Tuesday morning Stuart walked out of his house to find a small note stuck under the windshield wiper of his metallic-shale Audi saying, simply: *Bastard*. When their friends Austyn and Jed Jacobsen stepped out of a Szechwan restaurant with Stuart's wife Valerie and him after a nice dinner Wednesday evening, Stuart found a second not-so-small note stuck under his windshield wiper. *What next?* it inquired in a red scrawl. He balled it up and chucked it into the slushy street before Valerie could catch up with him. "Stupid advertisement," he told her when she looked like she might inquire about it. They spent Friday and Saturday at their cabin up on the shore of Lake

3

Superior near Beaver Bay and returned two hours ago to discover their house had been broken into while they were away. The only thing missing, so far as they could determine, was a single pillow from their bed. After the police left, a shaken Valerie headed off to keep a lunch date. Stuart drove here to calm down, clear his mind, and reflect. It isn't working. A new message has just appeared on his PDA. *Are we having fun yet?* it asks. Stuart is quite confident he knows the answer.

... DORK WITH THE HANDHELD THINKING?
Lara McLuhan, nibbling her thumbnail, finds herself
wondering four seats to Stuart's right, just sure
someone's going to walk into a shoe store and
purchase a pair of whatever those are without a man
in a clown mask holding a gun to your head and
threatening your children. Lara works at Forever
21 on the second floor and takes her role in what   5
she conceives of as The Great Retail Drama with
thin-lipped earnestness. Sixteen and two months,
if she puts on enough makeup and a tight sweater,
and if the lighting is fluttery, Lara can pass for
eighteen. She was born in Bloomington and will die
there. This knowledge fills her with extraordinary
pride because she knows her city is home to more
hotel rooms (6,800 of them) than downtown
Minneapolis and Saint Paul combined. Outside
you're always rushing to get somewhere, Lara feels,
yet when you're strolling through the Mall of
America there's so much to look at you relax.
Someone tried to make a mummy out of that lady
over there, wrapping her in eight thousand layers
of black shawls, and those things are rhinestones,
and the grottily zitty guy in the navy-blue what is
that a McDonald's uniform with cap three rows

behind her is wearing Converse All-Stars. In certain situations Converse All-Stars have their rightful place in the social fabric, but not when the fashion irony is totally lost on someone unaware he is living in a state of fashion irony. Lara leans back, surreptitiously evaluating her fellow filmgoers, the necessity for people like her in the world clear in her mind as the oceanfrost blueness of Nick Carter's scandalous eyes every time he sings to her from that awesome video, only her, about how the real story in every human relationship is the story of loss.

MIGUEL GONZALEZ AND ANGELICA ENCINAS
wait neither for the glary lights to dim nor the trailers
to flash awake before beginning to feel each other
up. They are fourteen and have snuck into the next-
to-back row on their first date. A chant is cycling
through Miguel's head: *Just my hand on her thigh, just
there, just like that, look, just my fingers moving beneath
her skirt, just the tips, just the slowness of them, just the*
heat of her skin, just that and nothing else, just the way
she smells, peppermint shampoo, just these things, just
these and nothing more, just here, just like this, just my
fingertips moving. Angelica, eyes closed, is far away
from Miguel's hand. She is imagining an establishing
shot in her very own private documentary: there
Miguel and Angelica are making out among all these
people settling in to their seats and the camera is
panning back and there is the AMC theater in which
they are sitting on the fourth floor of the Mall of
America tucked among thirteen others in which
hundreds of other people are settling into their seats
and the camera is panning back and there is the mall
itself frantic with thousands of other people frantic
with Christmas with dangling pink angels with
cotton-candy snowdrifts and the camera is panning
back and right through the roof and the parking

7

structures are receding through the graywhite blizzard and the city park and the hotels and the feeble car lights trembling and it is Sunday and here they are here Angelica and Miguel are and there could be other ways to express a beginning but this one is as good as any and these touches as good as any and so this must be desire sure why not this must be what they mean when they say that word.

00 : 00 : 04 : 12

AT THE BACK OF THE THEATER, in one of the
seatless spaces reserved for the handicapped,
slumps Zdravko Prcac in his motorized wheelchair.
Zdravko is wearing a baggy red, white, and blue
jogging suit with matching sneakers. Beneath it he
is wearing a one-piece style Depends with an
absorbent pad in the crotch area and no belts, tape,
or buttons. Eyes shut, chin on chest, suspended on   9
the whorling rim of sleep, Zdravko is semi-dreaming
of his dead wife Kosa, to whom he was married for
fifty-five years. When Kosa passed after a long battle
with a disease that turned her memories into water,
it felt as if a surgeon had visited Zdravko in the night
and extracted his lungs. He stopped eating, but his
nurse brought him to the hospital where the doctors
attached a tube beneath his collarbone to keep him
away from her. These days Zdravko's main goal in
life is to leave it. This is proving more difficult than
he anticipated. In the meantime, he strives to remain
invisible. A Serb charged with atrocities committed
at the Omarska camp, Zdravko fled through
Hungary to Austria in the final days of the war, from
Austria to America. He became eight different
people along the way, and is frightened he might
have caught immortality from a mosquito in the

Szeged train station one humid summer evening. Zdravko believes in certain international officials' eyes he still matters, but is mistaken. At the back of the theater, he semi-dreams he is sitting in his old living room with Kosa, reading the newspaper after work. It is winter. The electric fire is glowing. The heavy drapes are drawn. Kosa is knitting, only backwards. With each stitch she undoes, another memory drops away from her, a tuft of glassy milkweed.

BYRON METNICK, the scrawny usher scanning the audience from his post at the rear exit, doesn't like movies. He considers them serious wastes of time. They make him think too much, for one thing. Plus he read somewhere the majority of steady film patrons are between the ages of seventeen and twenty-nine with bachelor's degrees either in sight or in hand, and Byron despises every one of them. Last April, two months before graduation, he dropped out of Kennedy High, having learned exactly zip there except maybe how to type. Byron is totally down with his job here, though, because once a flick starts he gets to duck into the last row and catch a quick nap. After work, his friends and him cruise over to the park and smoke weed on the swings or in their cars and chill. Byron can't get baked at home because he still lives with his rents and his rents possess a veritable shitstorm of rules. Fridays and Saturdays, Byron sleeps late and returns to the mall in the afternoon. He gets high in his fourth-hand Dodge Colt in one of the parking structures, buys a Coke and jumbo fries at Malaysian Madness in the food court, and people-watches. After a while, everyone at the mall starts looking stunned like they've seen too much. If he waits long

11

enough, one of his friends eventually drifts by with news about where the best party will be that night. Byron then cruises over and smokes weed and chills until he finds himself nodding off in front of Road Runner cartoons in the basement. Meanwhile, Byron just likes looking. He finds the kids riding the Mighty Ax at the very point their sense of enjoyment wanes (eighty feet in the air, upside-down, teetering at the cusp of a plummet) particularly fucking hilarious. The way their eyes go all big. The way their jaws brace for impact.

LYDIA LARRABEE CARRIES a furry insect at the end of her name because that's how she remembers it and Lydia is this many old and her eyes are shut because there are boys and girls all over the world who see only with their fingers but Lydia went peepee and stepping out of the stall couldn't find her mommy in the crowded restroom and stepping out of the crowded restroom couldn't find her daddy 13 in the crowded lobby and now she thinks maybe she turned right thinking right was left but they went to Camp Snoopy this morning and splashed down the Log Chute into a cement mountain filled with puppets and in Cereal Adventure her favorite breakfast foods Cocoa Puffs Lucky Charms Trix came to life and Lydia petted a real live stingray in the petting pool at Underwater Adventure and this place smells like grownups' bottoms but if you squint just right it only looks like your eyes are closed but really you can see and her daddy told her there were thirty thousand plants and four hundred trees in Camp Snoopy and the world's biggest working LEGO clock in the Imagination Center was so pretty Lydia wanted to buy it and there was a red LEGO dinosaur with a gray belly and brown back and green blinking eyes and a baby LEGO dinosaur at

its feet so cute she wanted to buy that too and this
theater smells very small like grammy's apartment
on winter mornings when the radiator is running
and this wall feels very gray like a rug and Lydia
stands by it wishing she was blind and her hair long
like a princess's and full like golden smoke.

JEFF KOTCHEFF is engaged in an act of loathing. He pictures his seat, situated in the precise center of the theater, a foxhole, and the colorful boxes of candy, plastic container of chips and cheesy dip, cardboard carton stuffed with hotdog, jumbo-sized tub of buttered popcorn, and super-size Coke surrounding it sandbags. He has raised his armrests to accommodate his existence because when he concludes one meal his first thought is what he will have for a snack before the next. Jeff lives alone in a farmhouse on two-point-five acres of hilly land an hour and a half northwest of the city because he enjoys occupying space. That's what the universe is for, in Jeff's opinion: filling. He fists a wad of soppy popcorn into his mouth, takes a considerable slurp of pop, pushes his aviator glasses up on his nose, and glowers at the back of the head of the jewboy who just sat down in front of him. Jesus H. Christ. Six-fifty for a matinee and they remind Jeff of those extreme what do you call it bioforms he saw on the Discovery Channel last week that live in thermal vents at the bottom of the what do you call it Mariana Trench. This is why guns are so wonderful, but not as wonderful as small personal incendiary devices. Live and let live, believes Jeff, so long as you leave

15

my view corridor the fuck alone. When Jeff chomps down on his hotdog, relish and mustard ooze out the butt-end and glop onto his flannel shirtfront. Jeff is acutely indifferent. He is looking forward to a good love story with maybe Sarah Michelle Gellar or Gwyneth Paltrow in it. He could really use a first-rate romantic weeper right about now. Jeff Kotcheff wants to feel his heart tear. Jeff Kotcheff wants to cry his goddamn eyes out.

THREE ROWS BEHIND HIM, Vito Paluso chooses
an aisle seat. That way he can easily reach down and
shift the position of his crutches should someone
want to get by. Manipulating his bent bad legs into
place, he begins daydreaming about the video he is
making. Vito works as a security guard in the mall,
sitting in a cramped concrete room observing a wall
of surveillance monitors. When he locates a   17
disturbance, he phones his superior who walkie-
talkies down to his crew on the floor. Vito also
secretly scans the monitors for what he calls S.I.'s
(pronounced *sighs*), or Special Instants: those during
which tourists photograph each other. Or not
precisely those, but rather the ones immediately
following them, when people slowly stop smiling
after the shot has been snapped and you can actually
see their public masks soften and melt back into
everyday blandness, a gesture almost always
accompanied by a slight lowering of the head in a
miniature act of capitulation. Vito wants to capture
a hundred such moments, gray and grainy, slo-mo
and soundless, in a montage called *Where the Smiling
Ends*. Once a week, he dubs footage onto a VHS
tape he takes home, downloads it onto his computer,
and edits. For Vito, montage isn't a formalistic

technique. Continuity determined by the symbolic association of ideas between shots rather than literal connections in time and space is a philosophical principle. Vito believes[living is nothing if not a series of dissolves, superimpositions, odd juxtapositions, and unexpected cuts.] He would give anything to know someday his short will be shown at a film festival, except he is terrified by failure. He will therefore never finish the seven-minute-and-forty-four-second work that has already burned through nearly two years of his life.

SCANNING INDIFFERENTLY, Byron Metnick becomes aware of the cute little blind girl standing at the opposite end of row seven in the opposite aisle. She is feeling her way along the wall, obviously lost. Byron shrugs himself forward, shortcuts through a vacant channel of seats, puts on his professional nice-guy personality attributes, squats in front of her, and asks her where her mommy and daddy are. She opens her eyes, completely spooking him, and explains unperturbedly that she misplaced them. Exuding just the right mixture of responsibility and avuncularity, Byron takes her gummy hand in his and leads her out to the lobby where two anxious young parents, one fat and the other fatter, descend in a flutter of relief and guilt. On his way back in, he passes a huddle of overly enthusiastic theater personnel. In the center of the huddle floats one of those bald, wasted Make-A-Wish kids with her mother. Bald, wasted Make-A-Wish kids creep Byron out because they're both really gross and really pathetic at the same time. Suddenly bummed, Byron lowers his head, pretending not to notice, wide-arcs around them, and lurches into the darkening theater.

19

THE EXIT DOOR BEHIND Trudi Chan whuffs shut. The lights weaken. Trudi momentarily believes she is losing her sight. She crosses the left leg of her black business suit over the right, flicks off a fleck of invisible fluff, and exhales. She got into town late last night for a meeting near the airport first thing this morning. Afterward she took the shuttle in to pass a few hours before her flight to Chicago and another meeting first thing tomorrow morning. Trudi works for a private San Francisco aerospace firm run by a billionaire dot.commer researching malls to see what hermetically sealed one-stop living might tell us about how to construct orbital resorts in the future. Trudi Chan is in possession of a plethora of related arcana. She knows that the Del Amo Fashion Center in Southern California is larger than the principality of Monaco. That Tokyo boasts an underground shopping sprawl with forty-six movie theaters, fifteen hundred restaurants, fifteen discos, and six hundred ninety-nine mahjongg parlors. The mall in which she presently sits attracts more visitors annually than any other destination in the U.S., employs twelve thousand people, and can accommodate twelve-thousand-seven-hundred-and-fifty cars. Except Trudi isn't calling up any of

20

these bits of data right now. She is drifting in the soothing amniotic awareness that everyone around her is part of a much larger project than he or she suspects. This is because the cosmos, Trudi trusts, only appears chaotic, but is in reality an orderly place marked by harmony, synchronicity, and cooperation. All you have to do is look. All you have to do is pay attention.

THE EXIT DOOR BEHIND the huddle of overly enthusiastic theater personnel whuffs shut. The light in the lobby remains brash, one full wall being a bank of windows that overlooks the crisscross of verandas comprising the food court and, beyond, Camp Snoopy, a seven-acre skylit atrium wearing its battleship-gray filtration system and stanchions in plain view as if the architect had decided to turn a building inside out. In the center of the huddle floats the Make-A-Wish child with her mother. But the sickly little girl, buoyant in this luminous flash of public love, isn't really a sickly little girl. She is a twenty-eight-year-old dwarf named Magda Dorendorf who razors her head every morning, diets, wears cute pink skirts and cute pink sweaters with cute white cotton-ball clouds puffing across them, and smudges lilac eye-shadow beneath her eyes for that classic haunted chemo look. The tall thin woman standing beside her in a pair of scuba-goggle spectacles and platinum wig is Odele Krushnekov, Magda's lover. They have been on the road since October, leisurely driving from their crummy apartment in Hoboken to Los Angeles, where Magda plans to enter films. They have scammed their way through thirty-eight states. Their favorite stop so far has been in Darwin, Minnesota, home of the world's largest twine ball, a twelve-foot-in-diameter sphere weighing seventeen thousand four hundred pounds sheltered in its own Plexiglas-windowed hut. Magda doesn't know a tumor the size of a pencil eraser really *is* growing just beneath her left aureole. Nor will she discover it in time to decelerate its black yawning. In despair, Odele will join a women's religious cult whose members refuse to talk to other women, thereby boycotting their own gender and the pain it has caused them.

THE EXIT DOOR BEHIND Elmore Norman whuffs shut. The lights weaken. Elmore momentarily believes he is losing his sight. Mustached, slicked-back black hair feathered gray, married for more than twenty-two years to a gal named Harriett, Elmore swigs his Mountain Dew, wondering why he can't seem to get anywhere anymore. Elmore is up before seven every morning, at the mall by nine, firing up the grill at Malaysian Madness by ten. At one time or another he has cooked for eighteen people occupying this theater, although none would remember him. On his days off, he robs banks in the greater metropolitan area. What it is, is a guy's got payments. Elmore dresses in women's clothes and wig similar to Odele Krushnekov's and meets his buddy Tony, also disguised as a woman, in Tony's souped-up matte-gray Camero at the west parking lot. Neither of them owns a gun, so Elmore menaces the tellers with a crowbar he found in his basement. Elmore is lucky if him and Tony can split seven hundred bucks a pop. Two in three heists the greenbacks come with one of those hidden dye-packs that explodes as they jam, splattering the cash with indelible red ink. Elmore has robbed thirty banks so far. He doesn't know the one he will

24

attempt to knock off in two days will be his last. It will possess a lockdown bulletproof entrance that will trap him until the police arrive, crowbar notwithstanding. Tony, waiting across the street, will see what's gone down and book. The only thing Elmore will be able to show for his efforts will be a big-screen RCA television set he got a good deal on from that dago Juan Fernandez, which isn't fair, because Elmore already has one of those, plus the clicker doesn't work. He bought it last April for Harriett's birthday so she could watch her favorite show in style: *Cops*.

THE EXIT DOOR BEHIND the furry white puffer fish of a stray Persian cat whuffs shut. The lights weaken. The cat momentarily believes it is losing its sight. This doesn't especially trouble it. Nothing especially troubles it. In the course of its lifetime its name has been Buford, Bunny, Blanche, Bradford, Blossom, Boris, and Bathsheba. It has been unaware of them all, as it has of the fact it has enjoyed multiple owners, is a Persian, and once upon a time possessed something called a gender. Earlier today, as the cold atmosphere flaked away in silvery chips around it, it happened across an open door on a delivery dock and wandered through. At present it unknowingly sits beneath the seat of a bank robber, having entered a variety of perceptual stupor. A chemical randomly leaps a synapse behind its glacial blue eyes and it finds itself meandering into an aisle. Conscious only of its bladder plumping full in gradations, it halfheartedly scratches at the carpet, crouches, contracts some muscles, loosens others, and pees, forgetting in mid-act what it is doing, then remembering again. Done, it scratches at the carpet halfheartedly again, and, forgetting why it was scratching in the first place, finds itself meandering beneath the seat of a famous actor in disguise, ignorant that scientists from a parallel universe are trying to contact it telepathically from an invisible ship suspended three hundred miles over the Twin Cities. The scientists believe Persian cats comprise the most intelligent life form on the planet because they are plainly the most beautiful. This is one of the many reasons their civilization will collapse into rubble and fly wings in slightly fewer than three millennia.

TAKE, FOR INSTANCE, FIREFLIES, considers Trudi Chan. Fireflies share an internal metronome that sets the pace of their flashes based on what other fireflies in the vicinity are doing. And fads? Fads are nothing save flocks of people falling into step with each other without being told to do so. Even consciousness itself is the consequence of neurons firing in accord, a microscopic electrical symphony playing in ideal time behind our eyes. Unresponsive to points of historical interest, museums, or scenic views, whenever she finds herself in a new city Trudi vectors for the nearest mall. The outside strikes her as too disturbingly nineteenth century. She genuinely appreciates the glass doors at most mall entrances are purposefully tinted dark to make it seem continuously gloomy outside. Trudi wants to witness unsoiled concord in action. She wants to watch people dance a dance they don't even know they're dancing. She is interested in how these places concentrate our culture's favorite socially acceptable addictions--seeing, eating, and buying--beneath one roof in a single, collective, complexly meshed instant. How the drab exteriors announce nature's irrelevance. How malls have become the postindustrial equivalent of Japanese gardens:

28

everyone wants to find out what's in the next shop, around the next corner, up the next escalator. The more you look, the more you see. The more you see, the more you want. The more you want, the more you look. Malls are the only utopias that actually work, believes Trudi, spaces about promi ... The hollow sound of heavy breathing interrupts her reflections. She glances over her shoulder and spots two teens going at it three rows behind her. Trudi Chan's brain blanks.

WHAT STUART NAVIDSON failed to tell both the police and his wife is that he is almost positive whoever broke into his house also rearranged the poetry magnets on his refrigerator from puppet opens red door upon wolf sky to wolf puppet opens sky door upon red.

IN A FAKE GOATEE, tiny round wire-rimmed glasses, and schlumpy Irish tweed walking hat, Josh Hartnett kills time in the dark, wishing someone would recognize him. How famous can you really be, the idea nags and nags him, if you can throw people off this easily? The most important role any star plays is himself. He is known precisely for his well-knownness. So how much of a star can Josh Harnett be if no one around him can tell Josh Harnett is Josh Harnett trying not to look like himself? Tomorrow he will meet his buddy Matt Dillon less than a mile from Stuart and Valerie Navidson's cabin on the shore of Lake Superior to start shooting a murder mystery. Josh will play a serial killer with a sensitive, caring side revealed through his relationship with his paraplegic older brother, played by Matt, whom Josh will ultimately euthanize by feeding him into a giant wood chipper in an homage to that scene from *Fargo*, only with Matt still alive, saintly expression upon his face, as Josh, torqued by guilt, hefts him into the yowling, spitting maw. Guillermo Arriaga wrote the screenplay. Matt will direct. This will be Josh's most psychologically complex and demanding role so far, and one he hopes will confirm once and for all his wide range

31

as an actor for those dubious critics out there--even though, honestly, he has some issues with Matt playing his sibling, what with that horse jaw of his and head too big for his body. Born and raised in St. Paul, Josh has only lived in Hollywood for a couple years. He misses his parents and looks forward to hanging out with them and some of his old high school buddies during breaks from the shoot, and ... hey, what's that smell? Josh raising his chin. Sniffing tentatively.

THREE BLACK TEENAGERS sag in their seats two rows from the screen. "Girl," the first, Lakeesha Johnson, is saying on her cell phone, eying the lightshow before her through substantial glasses. Some wack shit is going down up there involving a skinny-assed whiteboy in some phat-up silks dangling off the bottom of a train. The train is speeding through countryside somewhere in one of them places with mountains and shit. "I'm *here*, girl. No. Uh-*uh*. I ain't there, those I gonna be there but I ain't yet. Uh-*uh*. I be on my *way* there soon this thing done. Now I be right where I's at ... " Her friends Chantrelle Williams and Desria Brown aren't paying attention to her conversation. They are acting on the instinctive urge they feel to anticipate this trailer's plot and save that foo up there fore he gets hisself into some *real* trouble. "Yo, yo, check it out," Chantrelle instructs him, right hand raised limply, forefinger and pinkie pointing. "You got to work harder, bitch, else you *dead*. Come on now. That right." The skinny-assed foo struggles under the carriage where he locates an unlocked trap door that magically leads him up into this juice first-class cabin. Rising, weary yet somehow sweatless, hair unspoiled, he pats himself off, relieved, unaware of the remarkably large blockish bro in a fly zoot suit all bling-bling with a meat cleaver in one hand looming in the shadows behind him. The bro steps forward. His teeth are gold. "Watch you *back*, fag!" Desria shouts. "Yo, what you thinkin'? You turn round or you be in some *serious* shit now, aw-ight? That nigga gonna OJ you ass. What he thinkin', Chantrelle, baby? What. He. *Thinkin'?*" "Fuck if *I* knows, girl," responds Chantrelle Williams. "Fuck if *I* knows ..."

PIERRE, THE MAN IN THE BLACK mackintosh
sitting directly behind Chantrelle, row three, seat
six, caught immortality from a mosquito in the
Szeged train station one humid summer evening in
1942. There is one insect in the world that carries
the virus and, unlike others of its species, it is
iridescent, immortal itself, and blinks into existence
on Mondays and Wednesdays. The rest of the week   35
it resides in a parallel universe where it dies every
sixteen hours. Pierre was on a mission for the French
Resistance to eliminate a high-ranking German
officer passing through Hungary when the mosquito
bit him. Pierre can no longer recall his own last name
because it has been so long since he used it. Back in
Paris, his job was to wait on a street corner at night
until another man in a black mackintosh identical
to his own approached him and whispered a coded
message as he strolled past. Pierre then walked to
another street corner several blocks away where
another man in a black mackintosh was waiting for
him, and Pierre, strolling past, would reiterate
verbatim what he had heard. Sometimes the
messages were vitally important. Sometimes they
were gibberish. Pierre never knew which were
which. Feet aching like a pair of upset hearts, he

sometimes waited rainy hours for his contact to appear. Pierre believes people are expecting him somewhere in the mall this very minute. He believes he should be somewhere he isn't, although he doesn't know where that place is. He knows he has nothing to tell the people waiting for him. No one has approached Pierre with a message, coded or otherwise, in more than sixty years. Every morning he wakes feeling anxious he has nothing to tell anyone anywhere on this loose planet.

THE STEM OF MIGUEL GONZALEZ'S brain becomes an electrical squall as his fingertips contact the crevice forming the intersection of Angelica Encinas's upper thigh and lower groin. The soft, miraculous nexus is damply warm. A centimeter more, and Miguel encounters the resistance of her cotton panties. He has imagined this instant hundreds of times over the last month and a half. It is just how he imagined it. He slips his forefinger beneath the hem and meets the first stiff curls of pubic hair. He brings to mind all the occasions he has pictured slipping his forefinger beneath this hem and closes his eyes to savor the sensation fully. Then there is an explosion on the screen so loud Miguel tastes tinfoil. Angelica, hot palm on Miguel's crotch, recoils.

37

A JAMES-BONDISH GUY is drinking champagne with this top-heavy woman in a dining car. Next he's attacked by a yakuza, thrown out a window, shinnies back in through a trap door, gets thrown out another window by a huge black man, clambers through a second trap door that leads, not onto the roof, as logic dictates, but into some submarine rapidly filling with water. Scrambling for air, he's shot out a torpedo tube, not into the ocean, but a pastel-blue swimming pool sparkling like a serene Hockney painting in a sunny pink-and-white resort. Currently he's surrounded by tiger sharks, one, of which just blew up. Blew up? This is precisely what Garrett Keeter despises about American films in particular and American culture in general. Both are just too fast and too noisy. How did he let Jaci talk him into this? All he wanted was to pick up some athletic socks, go home, and catch a nap. Despite that handful of dried mushrooms called his jetlagged mind, Garrett has to get busy tomorrow on his travel piece about Uganda. It's due in New York on Thursday. Ten days ago Jaci and he flew to Zürich, from Zürich to Cairo, and from Cairo to Kampala, where they hired a guide at the Sheraton to drive them eight hours southeast on increasingly narrow,

38

rutted, red-dirt roads into the mountains of Bwindi Impenetrable Forest. That night they stayed in a tented camp and at dawn were joined by four other trekkers, two trackers, and a dozen soldiers carrying machineguns to dissuade the local rebels from taking potshots at the tourist economy. They rode in back of a rickety troop carrier to the edge of a pasture, then hiked up a trail past thatched huts into brush so dense the trackers had to machete open paths grown over since the day before. Five sweaty hours, and they came across leaf beds marked with scat, then broke through into a clearing alive with gorillas. Mothers with babies. Young males playing among branches. A pot-bellied silverback reclining sprawl-legged against the trunk of a tree like an old drunk. It rose languidly, scratched itself, snorted, and bolted forward in a fake charge, halting fewer than eighteen inches from Garrett's face. Garrett averted his eyes and covered his teeth like the trackers instructed. Grunting, the gorilla inspected him meticulously. It was the most astonishing thirty seconds in his life. Garrett Keeter from Bloomington, Minnesota, was smelling a silverback's breath. It smelled exactly like ... what? Exactly like

UM, ISN'T THAT JOSH HARTNETT OVER THERE?
Jaci wonders. Nope. No way. What would a guy
like Josh Hartnett be doing in Blooming
bumblefucknowhere? Only … She smiles to herself,
clearing her head, and cozies once again into the
rhythms of the trailer unfurling before her.
Something just blew up. But what? Jaci missed it.
40 She was miles away, hanging in a state of gray
relaxation. She's almost certain the feature will be a
light romantic comedy starring Hugh Grant. Hugh
Grant or one of those other cute charming English
types, sophisticated, witty, boyishly vulnerable,
whose names are eluding her at present. How long
has she been sitting here? She isn't sure. This is
how jetlag works. Jetlag makes time smear. Jaci
reaches out for her husband's arm and pats it
contentedly, unaware this is the last significant
gesture she will perform in her life. In two hours
and forty-seven minutes, Garrett and she will die of
injuries sustained in a car crash on their drive home.
Yep, Jaci Keeter concludes, sneaking another peek,
proud of herself. No doubt about it. Look. That's
him, all right.

THE GUY IN THE FASTFOOD UNIFORM, soles of his Converse All-Stars propped against the back of Jaci's seat, is Celan Solen. Celan works at the concession stand. On his breaks, he picks a theater at random and sneaks in to catch a couple minutes of whatever happens to be playing. Although he has slipped into this one more than two-dozen times lately, he still isn't sure what this movie is about. 41 Sometimes it seems to be a historical drama set in the nineteenth-century South, others all aging Bruce Willisesque action-adventure. Once Celan strolled in just as a college hottie in a skimpy bra and panties got disemboweled by a man in a featureless white mask. In the end, though, it doesn't really matter. Put Celan in front of a flickering screen and he's happy. Celan is not especially into narrative, not especially into character, and he feels pretty much anyone can tell one of the nine extant plots in the world. The trick for Celan Solen is always the how and the why of the telling. What he is concerned with is the mind in motion as it is disclosed by celluloid. For him the dominant metaphor for good film derives from the idea of The Persistence of Vision, where the human brain retains images the eye receives for a fraction of a second longer than the eye actually records them. If it didn't, we would all go crazy with the jump-cut awareness of blinking. What we see in blinking's place is an unending optical illusion: a coherent, continuous version of reality. To record a single fixed photograph on a frame, the camera's shutter remains open about one-thirtieth of a second. The shutter exposes sixteen of those images every second in silent film, twenty-four in film with sound. One second of exposed silent film therefore contains only sixteen-thirtieths of a second of exposed action and fourteen-thirtieths of nothingness between frames. Which is to say, Celan continually delights in reminding himself, when we watch a movie in a theater we spend as much as half our time in the dark without knowing it ... and yet we make complete sense of the shattered light-blips we perceive. Life flies at us in bright splinters. We turn them into significance. If Celan Solen could somehow capture such an understanding in a film of his own making, he would die satisfied. No matter how hard he tries, however, such an accomplishment will always remain just beyond his grasp. He will strive for it nearly twenty years, but gain international fame only after abandoning his quest and creating a tiny, vapid, forgettable love story steeped in 1970's nostalgia that will cause vast numbers of viewers to weep uncontrollably during the last twelve minutes by heaping cliché atop cliché in a manner so mercilessly calculated that Celan Solen will never forgive himself. He will stop directing and, a millionaire in his mid-forties, return to his roots behind the glass counter out front because for him right here is what home should always feel like.

BIG-BONED COSMETOLOGIST Betsi Bliss accidentally touches elbows with Celan Solen, reflexively twitches free, and whispers a polite apology. She supposed she was watching a preview for a picture until the tall, dark, handsome secret agent climbed the ladder out of that pool into the murky belly of a flying saucer sweating ooze down its unnervingly organic walls. Then she almost stopped supposing altogether. Events had certainly gotten ... well, *odd*, hadn't they, and Betsi has never been fond of oddness. Oddness is far too odd for Betsi Bliss. The secret agent produced a bottle of green mouthwash, smiling an urbane smile and raising his prize aloft among delighted tentacled space creatures with wobbly purple heads. The space creatures clapped, even though they possessed no hands, and it dawned on Betsi that she had been watching a commercial masquerading as an SF picture masquerading as a secret agent picture. Not that such a recognition made her feel much better. Betsi loves only two things in life: applying just the right amount of rouge on a woman's cheekbones for that wholesome natural look, and praising Jesus Christ Our Lord and Savior. Every Saturday, Betsi and her husband Bobby (presently contemplating the sign in the window of the Chapel of Love one floor below: "Eat, Drink, and Remarry--Ceremonies Start @ $269") attend the clapboard Church of the Blessed Roadkill. Preacher Pete, rotund man with a flaming white beard like a frozen white blast, tells them how best to serve their Redeemer. Betsi listens to every word, sometimes taking notes in a small spiral bound notebook. One, she once wrote, you got to give Him everything you have because the Redeemer is all about Total Sacrifice with capital letters. B, you got to *believe* right down to that part of your tummy where fear and desperation dwell. In conclusion, you got to feel Him inside you as if He had set up a tiny radio in the middle of your forehead. During the week, Preacher Pete crisscrosses the county in his Ford pickup, living off what the Lord leaves him along the roadsides because the Lord sustains and maintains and contains but never refrains because He knows best because He sees the whole picture while we see ... we see, it occurs to Betsi with a joyful shock, only the trailers, and then only if we're looking real hard so we can figure out what's really a trailer and what's only a commercial masquerading as a trailer. From puberty's onset, Betsi Bliss has suffered from what Preacher Pete diagnosed as the Strange and Holy Malady of Wickedness Recognition. In times of vague distraction, Betsi becomes aware of itching sensations across her back accompanied by the impression of fluttery kisses. When she investigates the site of irritation in a mirror, she discovers an irruption of stitch-like lesions that, upon closer examination (and interpretation by Preacher Pete at their private sessions on Wednesday afternoons), spell out the chief transgressions she has committed by the very act of being alive in this World of Shame. Betsi Bliss believes her disease is a blessing in disguise. It's always nice, holds Betsi Bliss, to find out what your sins are without having to think too hard.

FRED QUOCK'S THOUGHTS REFUSE to walk in a straight line. A pudgy pilot for Northwest Airlines, Fred sports a vestigial salt-and-pepper mustache and vestigial mouth. He is here to pass a palmful of hours before his flight to Atlanta. On the balcony overlooking Camp Snoopy, Fred phoned his wife, Carla, in Salt Lake City, to tell her he loved her. Fred and Carla were high-school sweethearts. For more than thirty years, they conceived of each other less as husband and wife than socially adept friends. When this flick is over, Fred will meet Pablo Tati, a flight attendant twelve years his junior, in America's Original Sports Bar. They will share several syrupy drinks, then take separate shuttles to the Country Inn and Suites where Fred will rent a room on the fourth floor, don a Snagglepus outfit, and boink Pablo senseless. Fred never feels as alive as when dressed as a Furvert, his life rich with secrets and deception. He is feeling exceptionally alive today. Besides imagining Pablo's cute doughy potbelly that reminds him of an enormous plucked chicken breast, Fred is busy gloating about winning an all-expenses-paid trip to the Happy Trails Dude Ranch near Bozeman, Montana. He doesn't remember having entered the twenty-five-words-or-less contest, but

46

he enters ones like it all the time. What Fred doesn't
know is that Gordo Jarmush, his ex-lover, is playing
a prank on him to punish Fred for being such a
sadistic, insensitive bastard. The Happy Trails Dude
Ranch closed three years ago. Fred will soon learn
how little there is for a weekend cowboy in pressed
jeans, bolo tie, ten-gallon hat, and sharp-toed
rattlesnake boots in Bozeman other than wandering
the dull main drag, waiting for the next three
minutes to pass away, and then waiting for the next
three minutes to pass away again.

CLAUDE AND MOUCHE MÉLIÈS, the couple
directly to Fred's right, give the impression of being
faintly bewildered inhabiting this theater. Last July
they invited over a colleague of Mouche's at the
University and his wife for drinks. Claude and
Mouche only glanced at each other when the man
and woman showed up carrying overnight bags.
Claude cheerfully ushered them into the living room
while Mouche fetched scotch-and-sodas. The first
hour slow-faded into the second. Next, it was half
past eight and no one had mentioned dinner yet.
Feigning casualness, Mouche slipped into the
kitchen, rifled through the fridge and pantry for
foodstuffs, and returned to offer everyone club
sandwiches. Afterward, the woman excused herself
and disappeared upstairs. The man found a novel
on the bookshelf in Mouche's office, took a seat in
her leather recliner, and read. If Claude remembered
correctly, it followed the thoughts of a number of
people watching a musical extravaganza until,
unexpectedly, a bomb went off in the playhouse near
the end and everybody died. Eventually Claude,
who had been washing dishes, set out in search of
Mouche to discuss their options. Instead, he
discovered the woman sprawled on their bed

upstairs, dress hiked over her waist, sleeping. Her overnight bag was open on the oak armoire. Claude backed out and continued his search, after some time finding Mouche snoring lightly on a couch in the guest bedroom. He undressed and lay down on the rug on the floor beside her. Next morning, he awoke to the scent of pancakes. The man had made a delicious breakfast. That afternoon and evening wafted by, but the man and the woman didn't leave. A week evaporated, then two. July blanched into August. More than once Claude and Mouche had to confess privately their guests were pleasant housemates, the atmosphere generally cordial. They celebrated Labor Day together, collected before the TV to watch the Thanksgiving's Day parade, drove into the country to cut down a bushy tree for Christmas. This morning Mouche awoke with a slight sinus cold and remained indoors while Claude shoveled the accumulating snow off the back patio. When he tried to enter the house at lunchtime, he found the side door locked. Puzzled, he walked around front. That door was locked as well. He rang the bell, waited, rang again. No one answered. He tried several windows. No luck. He cupped his hands and peered in. The house was dark. He heard footsteps behind him and turned. It was Mouche. She walked right past him, saying over her shoulder: "Come on, let's get going." "Get going?" Claude asked, looking back at the side door. "It's locked," Mouche said. "The windows, too. I'm hungry." And so, after a slight hesitation, they cut through the yard, climbed over the fence, and, hand in hand, strolled up the street past many houses in the neighborhood that had been taken over and some that had not. Before long, they found themselves here. They haven't seen a movie in six months. Between them they possess fewer than a hundred dollars. They don't know where to go. They don't know what to do. They feel like candles. They feel like someone is trying to blow them out.

ELMORE NORMAN TAKES another sip of
Mountain Dew and is transported to a faraway
desert land. A crusader on horseback, he slays a
dragon the dimensions of a school bus. The dragon
is covered with shimmering scales, each comprised
of a three-dimensional photograph of a possible
future. In a cave guarded by genie, Elmore comes
across an exact tiny silver replica of his own house
among piles of gold. In the replica, tiny versions of
Harriett and him watch a tiny big-screen television
set. They are sitting side by side on a tiny couch,
sharing a tiny bowl of ice cream. They look
overweight and they look bored. After solving a
complicated riddle posed by the genie, Elmore
marries a firm-breasted Nubian slave and fathers
eight children by her. He grows old. Two of his
children are killed in an earthquake, one by
pestilence, one by war. His Nubian wife leaves him
for another woman. His friends in Minneapolis
forget him and move on with their lives. Elmore
loses his possessions when he bets the sun will rise
the next day, but it doesn't. Beaten down, his health
declines, his organs give out, disease makes a meal
of his body. Lying alone on his deathbed in a dark
tent stinking of rotten canvas, Elmore's vision dims.

Somehow he always thought the end would be a lot worse than this. It is bad, certainly, but somehow he always thought it would be a lot worse. Closing his eyes for the last time, aware that every man begins his life as many men but dies as only one, he swallows, and is back in his seat in the multiplex, sipping his Mountain Dew. It strikes Elmore Norman that million-to-one odds happen nearly nine times a day in Manhattan.

A NEW THOUGHT ARRIVES behind the considerable forehead of Leon Mopati, the Unitarian minister occupying the seat just in front and to the right of the one occupied by Elmore. Every culture, goes the thought, gets the architecture it deserves. Leon looks like a black Vincent van Gogh with both ears still intact. Born and raised the second son of a diamond baron in Botswana, Leon came to America eighteen years ago to study theology at the University of Minnesota, fell in love with the foliage and snowblaze, and never looked back. Saada, his wife, a lawyer, is presently shopping. What a terrible place to be, thinks Leon: shopping. Unending space crowded with an excess of sameness. Makes you feel lost even when you're not. Distracted. Unmoored. Like on that hot white day among the broken stones. Whiff of baked dust in the air. How signature structures bare a society's what. Lusts. The for example. Pyramids of Giza. Cheops a thirteen-acre rock garden to the sun. Or the skeletal luminescence of a Parisian train station at midday, hosanna to the Mechanical Age. The street enters the house. The house enters the future. The future moved from Paris to Rome that spring. Walking the ruins of the Forum with her. The hot white day, the shadeless

53

solid chronicle. How happiness happened between one footfall and the next. First mall, really, if you stop to think about it. Nine-hundred-year old center of commerce, faith, and politics the Middle Ages turned into a cow pasture. Nice work, guys. Her floppy white tourist hat turned her into a beekeeper, every step they took an act of imagination among the maplessness. But ours? Fritz Lang's nightmare, only in color. The corrugated ceilings. The blah beige. The jade. The cinnabar highlights. Slackfaced teens hunkering against banisters playing with their taffy gum. Whose home? Farewell to an. How we touched hands simply because touching hands was the right thing to do. On the path among clicking cameras, chattering tourist guides, those low rails to keep you from the valuable rubble. Irregular manhole-cover rocks felt like walking on frozen waves. Reminding, trying to remind, of a white that was different. There we were in Italy one day in the light of an aging afternoon among the gnarly nearly leafless trees. Olive. Olive or fig or what olive or fig trees should resemble in the mind's eye. Narrow leaves. Stalky like bamboo. But here? The great Schulzian omphalos. His very own cathedral. Our Blessed Cartoonist of the. No wonder F. Scott Fitzgerald was born in this place. Where else could he have turned up? How we blinked and were in Rome, my beekeeper and me, the light working like atomic bleach upon the bone stones around us. Sitting to catch our breaths on a broken column. It was let us call it April. April or May. Not a travel brochure in motion, not a commercial for something or other, not a preview up there. No. Just some dumb visuals for the Xbox. Certain devices we use every day, that is, having become supernatural.

54

September 24, 1896. That's it. Get a couple of gigs under your skin, and all you want is more. F. Lang Fritzgerald Day. Snug human scale tucked into a vast, fast, rattling hive. Paul Bunyan in drag. Saint Paul, mythic matherfother of Midwestern clearcutters, unmoved mover of our hygienic fountains and blindbright atriums, stained glass and raggybaggy costumes. Our belonging. Our community. Like the story. That one. You know. The Great Lakes boy whose family transplanted him early one autumn from one burb to the next. Every day he mounted his little red bicycle to pedal the concrete seas five miles to his favorite mall. Because *that* was home, you see. His being a part of. The Penelope. The place. Same principle with any musical you simply have to see more than once: ritual sing-along to the same singsongs everyone else in the audience rituals to: excess of sameness: videlicit *home*. Because sleep is our reward for having to stay awake so long. Twenty years for him, wasn't it? Ithacant. Ithacan. Ithaca. Our mindwharf. Because Leon Mopati believes he may have read somewhere the film which is about to commence will contain musical bits in it, but oddly. Over fivehundred stores. Minnesot-ah! Bow Wow Meow. Count Your Blessings. Your what? But not one label in the Forum explaining where the hell you were. Just thingless names on baby plaques. Julian Basilica. Temple of the Vestal Virgins who kept the sacred flame fired. Had to remain chaste for what was it thirty years. Or else. Buried alive. Dirtmouths. Where did language go when our backs were turned? The lullaby. The lament. The requiem. Farewell to an idea. The hot white day. The broken stones. The conjuring. The surprise Leon Mopati feels at least once every week, the one he is feeling right now, that he fell in love with his own wife for the first time during that uneventful stroll among the ruins after almost a decade and a half of being married.

MOIRA LOVELACE LOOKS LIKE a flautist in her fifties: short, prim, stringy. She reminds Leon, one seat to her right, of a cubist painting. Weekdays, Moira teaches algebra at Kennedy High. Looking out on her students, she sees a classroom crammed with space aliens. She cannot understand their lingo. She cannot understand their clothing. What they listen to too loudly through their headphones may be many things, but none of them is music. Every Saturday evening Moira stays at home and makes sex videos of herself in her king-size bed, sheets silk leopard like in spy thrillers from the sixties. Sometimes with one hand she employs a pink dildo that reminds her of a small pink torpedo. Sometimes she employs plastic bags and smeary makeup. The general impression is one of a messy clown asphyxiating, naked. Moira has learned a lot about cinematography over the years. How it is almost impossible to produce a movie single-handedly. How a whole evening can be devoted to a worthy sixteen-second clip. Every Sunday Moira stays in, making copies of her video, packing each in a plain brown envelope. On her way to school every Monday morning, she mails the envelopes to strangers across the country. Moira locates their

57

names in phonebooks at the library. She thinks of her sex videos as love letters to the world. They put a crackle into lives of people she will never meet and punish her for creating them in the first place. A discreet grin tightens across her lips as Moira Lovelace pictures who may be thinking about her this very second in Omaha, Nebraska, and how.

EVERYONE ELSE LAUGHS after that gal up there whomps that feller on the head with the teddy bear so Ida and Johnny Ray Jarboe laugh too cuz that must mean it's real funny what the heck they's here to have a good time. Saved two years drove all night from Pikeville Kentucky with Grammy and the kids in the back to whoop it up a little that's just what they's gonna do. After breakfast at Sbarro they drop Grammy at the Super 8 drop Little Johnny Ray and Betty Sue and Susie Lynn and Lynna Ann with her rag-baby at Underwater Adventure give them a hundred bucks tells them to meet at the West Parking Exit in Tennessee at closing time don't forget now Tennessee. Back home Ida works as a waitress at Bob's Big Boy it's okay nice people good tips. Johnny Ray is between jobs so he helps his Uncle Wilgus raise a little juanita in the woods back of his cabin. That's where he done had his first visitation one night out harvesting all by his lonesome. Bright triangle appears outta nowheres and them voices start going at it in his head hens in a chicken coop Johnny Ray all dizzy like as if he's walking on a slant. Turns out they's got five things to say in our language just five that's all and they says them over and over. *Other side. Wooden song. Do it yourself. Sooner or later.* *Hammer.* Johnny Ray he beelines fer home wakes Ida tells her what he done seen. She says that dog won't hunt cuz you know women then she says maybe it will. Ida reckons the message may be some kinda secret code or whatnot like as they have in *Mission Impossible.* *Sooner or later* they's coming to our plane to tell us something cuz we's so goddamn ignorant about most everything no shit got *that* straight. So us earthlings got to pick up a *hammer* build a *do it yourself* landing site to help guide them in which is what Ida and Johnny Ray are doing you bet. Only to get the coordinates they got to listen to a *wooden song* or you know music box anybody can figure that one out. Course Ida and Johnny Ray sorta thought it would be plain when you walked into the San Francisco Music Box Company with them spacemen running a covert operation down there on behalf of their alien empire which particular music box was the right particular music box but they was skunkpiss wrong. Mind you over the years Johnny Ray come to understand them voices ain't got just those five things to say in their native language neither no way. They can chaw about all manner of things if they wants to sure who can't only they speak when they's got something to say and they's got something to say maybe three four times in their entire lives. Otherwise they's fine jes thinking to each other with their brainwaves only not too much cuz communicating as they see it is nothing except a invasion of privacy. So here Ida and Johnny Ray sit watching a show waiting for another sign. That's what's so great about this great country of ours. Body can walk three miles inside the Mall of America and never step into a store can spend ten minutes in each and three days later you know

60

what? Three days later you's still ambulating no finish line in sight what a thing ain't nothing like it in the whole wide world nope that's the Lord's honest truth sure is.

FASTIDIOUS ANDERSON BATES, the prematurely
gray contract lawyer in row seven, seat two, wishes
the crackers in front of him would at least wash their
hair. He can smell it from here. Anderson works out
of his split-level in Woodbury. To stretch his legs, he
sometimes rises from his desk and wanders from
room to room in his house, parting the curtains and
studying his neighbors' homes for signs they are out:
empty driveways, drawn shades, unclaimed mail.
Anderson keeps careful records. Hands in pockets,
he then casually strolls over (Ellen, his wife,
volunteers at the local library four mornings a week),
lets himself in, and has a poke around. He wears
surgical gloves. He almost never takes anything. If
he does, he makes sure it is an object no one will
miss. A cheap pen. A handful of AAA batteries
from a kitchen drawer full of them. He will often
tidy atomizers and trays atop an armoire or products
on a refrigerator shelf. Often he just likes to look.
Anderson envisions himself an anthropologist
interested in how other tribes live. He is especially
drawn to bathroom cabinets. The information
housed in pill bottles, spray cans, and salves makes
Anderson's head light. On occasion he likes to touch.
He likes to feel other people's property in his palms,

62

knowing hours later his neighbors will handle the same objects he just handled. He likes to rearrange things so his neighbors can't tell whether they have been rearranged or not. He imagines the slight sensation of disorientation his neighbors will feel and believes it will do them good. Those crackers in front of him break into laughter again and Anderson finds himself speculating about why toenails grow. They accomplish zero in life except the ceaseless increase of proteinaceous contamination. But why?

BETTY AND JERRY ROEMER, retired middle-school teachers in matching pale blue jogging suits, have been members of the Mall Walking Club for Seniors since Monday, August 11, 1992, the day the doors opened. They assume the teens gathered in discrete herds throughout this place are making fun of them behind their backs for being old and odd looking as they power-stroll by. Betty and Jerry are right. Of course, it's only natural. No teen can connect the dots leading from his or her own flesh to Betty's and Jerry's. To keep their brains breathing, they are taking a continuing education course on the history of movies at Normandale Community College. According to their professor, the film they have come to see deals with the *fluidity of subject positions.* They have no idea what the *fluidity of subject positions* means, but are looking forward to finding out, so long as it doesn't involve violence, nudity, foul language, or subtitles. Although the attitudes of their bodies suggest they may not know each other, they are participating in the identical thought: the comforting thing about malls is the comforting thing about fastfood franchises: they are essentially the same wherever you go. Absentmindedly kneading his earlobe with thumb and middle finger, Jerry sees himself lose balance next week and tumble down the stairs in their duplex. It won't hurt. For a second it will feel like gliding, then it will sound like a wetly cracking pencil. And then the lights will go out, just like that. Betty will follow three months later in her sleep because of what she will perceive as a violation of a fundamental filmic principle: the common sense philosophy implied by edited shots transitioning smoothly from one to another. Betty will brook none of it, none whatsoever.

1. CYNTHIA MORGENSTERN, one seat behind and right of Jerry Roemer, wants to love Cary Grant, only in black and white.

2. Conceivably there are special contact lenses for such a purpose.

66   3. Fat is horrifying because it makes you look like a bullfrog version of yourself. Fat reminds Cynthia of something washed up after a storm on a tropical beach.

4. Let your heart be a raisin.

5. Germs are filthy blizzards blowing through your bloodstream.

6. Cynthia wants to dwell in a silent film. Sans other actors.

7. Be still.

8. Cynthia believes in therapy through television watching. Treasure the angel within you. Remember we all awaken to the brightness of the same sun.

9. Don't touch your armrests. Your seat cushion. Don't touch your face.

10. Let your surgical mask do its work.

11. Recently Cynthia has realized life is probably the thing that arrives in ten-minute portions disturbed by commercials.

12. Your body is a smaller theater situated inside a bigger theater situated inside a bigger theater.

13. Theaters are places where outside time and space go away.

14. Cynthia likes theaters.

15. It is dark. Remain calm. This will all be over soon.

CHEST A BURNING BUSH, Vladislav Dovzhenko stares at the movie screen without understanding what he is hearing. This isn't because he doesn't know English. Even though raised in central Kazakhstan in an area Russian rocket scientists once used as their sandbox, Vladislav has lived in this country five years. No: he can't concentrate because six days ago on a dirt road near the Salton Sea he made the biggest haul of his career. Back in his apartment half a mile away, sealed in a large Ziploc Sandwich Bag buried beneath a potted rhododendron, rest thirty-two Krugerrands. This is more wealth than Vladislav has possessed at any time during his nineteen years. What he likes most about the Russian mafia is it is the kind of organization that will shoot you just to see if the gun works. Vladislav doesn't know that the Centurion safe he helped liberate from two terrified Mexicans in an Army-surplus Jeep seventeen miles northwest of Calipatria belonged in April 1986 to a man named Anatoly Dyatlov, chief engineer at Chernobyl the day its reactor expired in a plume of lethal steam. The Russian mafia hired six unsuspecting teens, Vladislav among them, to pull off the heist because the Krugerrands are shot through with radiation.

On his drive to Minneapolis, where he plans to lay low, work out at Los Campeones Fitness Center, and pick up easy American chicks at local bars, he wore six Ziploc Sandwich Bags distended with his irradiated booty glued to the inside of his thighs beneath his shapeless pants just in case a cop pulled him over. At rest stops he walked like Boris Karloff in *Frankenstein*. Seven years, and he will be sterile. Nine, and he will lose his eyesight. But now, one seat behind and to the right of Cynthia Morgenstern, Vladislav Dovzhenko gloats and gloats.

THE UNSHAVEN, TROLLISH TEEN dressed in black jeans, black button-down shirt, and Bolle sunglasses two seats to Vladislav's right is conducting an imaginary interview with himself. Yeah, um, Brandon Bazin is saying to Barbara Walters behind his eyelids, so like the camera is supposively rolling and all? Okay. So. Zondi. ...? Yeah. Just Zondi. Fuck the parental-naming thing, dog. That kinda shit is all about like social control and whatevuh. ...? Yeah. Grand Rapids. ...? No. The, um, the other Grand Rapids. ...? Kind of, but not really. I knew I had what it took since like forever, pretty much. ...? The art establishment is all like: you don't have any "talent." I'm all like: wassup with *that*? ...? Communications. ...? What? ...? Normandale Community College. ...? Sucked. They're all like: you flunk. I'm all like: whatevuh. Which is when I meet Mongo at the Fringe Festival. He introduces me to AIDS. ...? Arts In Denial & Shit. Which it deals with like stuff that like denies it's like art? Which gives me this idea for my own magum okus. ...? What? ...? Eighteen. ...? So I'm all like: fuck the commodrification of images, know what I'm saying? I won't like create a fucking thing for the rest of my life. *That's* my like project. ...?

70

What? Three-point-two mil. ...? *Not* doing
something being the like something I'm doing, know
what I'm saying? It's a, um, statement. ...? I dunno.
What do *you* think it means? ...? Really? Huh ...
So I'm all like ... ...? Three-point-two. Yeah. ...?
Listen to music, mostly. Surf the tube. ...?
Nickelodeon. Lotta fly shit in SpongeBob is like
strictly for adults, know what I'm saying? ...?
Lately? Thinking about taking up teaching. ...?
Yeah. I'm all like: maybe it's time to give something
back ...

ED BERGMAN IS FIFTY-EIGHT years old but he doesn't know how old he is. He is an auto mechanic with three grandchildren but he doesn't know who he is. Ed just woke up a second ago in an uncomfortable chair, row four, seat six, behind a big-eared man in a black mackintosh and is awash with worry someone was supposed to pick him up here but hasn't or maybe Ed should be somewhere else but isn't. It occurs to him there is a good chance he is drifting through deep space inside a capsule with a television screen set into the wall where the porthole should be and mistaking what is on the screen for what is really happening to him. Next he cannot remember having just had that thought. Ed wishes every Malaysian Madness franchise would provide a selection of serotonin reuptake inhibitors on the menu but he would also settle for simple painkillers. Ed cannot fathom why certain people are bent on concealing the fact there are no animals in Barnum's Animals Crackers nor goldfish in Pepperidge Farm Goldfish. Sometimes he can see his ideas. Sometimes they look like flaky little white wedges of angel-food cake crumbling in a large black mouth. Ed can feel someone grinding them up and swallowing them down. Sometimes if he listens very closely Ed Bergman can hear gastric fluids fizz, slosh, and gurgle around his thoughts exactly like a threat.

NIGHTS, LARA MCCLUHAN TAKES classes at Normandale Community College. She graduated high school a year early and wants to earn an associate degree in business so she can run her own upscale shoe store. Her schedule allows her two free afternoons a week. Sundays she treats herself to a movie like this. Tuesdays she drives to a warehouse 74 across town to star in bukkake videos. Seventy-five men cum on her face and in her hair during a shoot. Because she can pass for eighteen, no one at Face Value Productions asks Lara any questions. One of the other girls told her in ancient Japan women cheating on their husbands were tied up in the middle of town and humiliated like this. It doesn't concern Lara one way or the other. Bukkake is good money. The hours are reasonable. Sometimes between shoots she catches up on her homework. But Lara doesn't like the taste much. It reminds her of snotty Brie cheese mixed with Ajax. When she Googled it, she was relieved to discover it contains nothing more than ninety-five percent water with traces of sugar, vitamin C, and zinc mixed in. Plus there are only twenty-five calories per load. Passing time on her knees, occasionally in a girls-school uniform, occasionally in a pair of schoolmarm glasses, occasionally with her wrists chained in her lap, Lara likes to shut her eyes, listen to all the cute little slupslapping sounds going on around her, and imagine the cleancut Republican financial advisor ten years older than she whom Lara is determined to marry by the time she is twenty-three. His name will be something in the leafy suburban neighborhood of Christopher or Brian or David. Christopher or Brian or David will enjoy the missionary position with the lights off. Lara and he will produce three remarkably fair-haired children with high IQs and enormous self-esteems. After making love, side by side in bed, Lara will ask Christopher or Brian or David to tell her the same story he always tells her, the one she read someplace but forgot where, as if it really happened to him: the one about that azure autumn morning he was on the forty-second floor of the North Tower when he looked up from his desk and saw a Boeing 767 getting bigger and bigger through the window. Without thinking, Christopher or Brian or David began to run. Down on the street, he peered up the very instant Nick and Jim, two of his colleagues who had always hated each other, always done nothing but snipe and bicker, leaped from a gaping burning rectangle on the sixty-fifth floor. They were holding hands. This future memory always makes Lara feel simultaneously patriotic and romantic, causing a diminutive smile to form upon her perfect lips at just the right time.

... BUT, LEON CONSIDERS, PICTURE THIS: two angels walking through the light of that aging Italian afternoon. The ruins. The dusty olive trees. Olive or fig. Or, better: through your what. Lush garden. At dawn. Yes. That's it. The beekeeper asleep somewhere above you. The day a motionless ocean you will cross. Again. Rowing through the minutes, one home to another. Morning fog suffused by peach sunshine. Coffee and apples. These are your angels walking arm-in-arm, faces white light splashed on broken columns. Picture this, but picture it taking place in another dimension. An antispace thought. I have spent my life asserting the possibility they are there. Here. Here, of course, and not here. Call it the dynamics of metaphor. The way they. Sweet berries. *Als ob.* The German form of hope. How, I want to ask, can you prove they're not? That's the interesting. Believing, we all feel far from the grave, and if you look and don't see them, I tell you they're invisible. If you listen and don't hear them, I tell you they walk on air. They don't breathe. Take a photograph. Go on. This is your garden before you, your time behind you, yet all you will discover is saffron incandescence. Floppy green pancake leaves. Bright red flowers, fist-sized hearts

76

pulsing on stems. We live by the bluest reason, devoid of angels, you say. They had how many? Six limbs. Like insects. Rapture bugs. Produce a recording. Make it the highest quality. You hear birds chirping in the underbrush. A distant airplane hanging over a patchwork of houses. Perhaps even your own embarrassed cough in the background, proving only your own one-eyed existence. That's it. That's all. The ways we miss our lives are life. But that's enough. Enough and not enough. How do you know the photograph hasn't been retouched? The recording altered? When did angels become, like all words, somehow less than themselves? Let us say they have gone home. Let us say that. How do you know they haven't? God Himself left the planet in alarm. Without even bothering to say goodbye. Packed virtue in His valise and vamoosed. The hotel instead of the hymns. Leaving those who write to forget for the rest of us. How do you know you didn't miss them by a millisecond? A millennium? Take an x-ray. Go ahead. Set a trap. Hide with me behind that row of Queen Mother plums for an hour. A Mediterranean of bluely reasonable days. Like Sicily: land of pregnant men and manly women squat as Doric columns. We stayed in a pensione there whose name I forget whose brochure boasted, among other amenities, *one beach umbrella for hiving unity.* My beekeeper and me. What did it mean? *Als ob.* But quick: *behind you.* They've been standing there the whole time, celestial chameleons. You turn and they dissolve in your turning. Their soft hands of light are a motion. Maybe this time. Maybe this one. You can almost smell them, can't you? The fresh morning. The oranges. The opportunities ...

UNTIL TWO DAYS AGO, Arnold Frankenheimer worked for the biggest asshole in the world. Designing the website for the guy's start-up health-food company was a McJob like other McJobs Arnold had had: eight hours in a nondescript cubicle followed by the evening with his girlfriend, Heather, their new baby, Kayla, and maybe a little pot before bed. Arnold didn't mind much. Then he did. After lunch Friday, he emailed his boss his resignation letter. It said, simply: *Fuck you very much. I quit.* Arnold then linked the website to the Face Value Productions one and walked. Now his girlfriend and daughter have to eat. Rent is due next week. Arnold is screwed. This morning he drove to the mall in his Honda Civic and found a seat at The Crepe Stand for an earnest think. Once upon a time, it struck him, sitting there, a sense of meaning derived from what you produced. If you were an arrow maker in Germany, your last name would be Fletcher. These days meaning derives from what you consume. You eat at cafés with which you want to be associated and pick your identity off a rack at The Gap. In the midst of this thought, Arnold decided to smash his car into the side of the Mall of America at forty miles an hour. Arnold doesn't want to die. Far from it.

78

He wants to make available to himself and his new family a certain amount of insurance capital. This is how he will do it. First he will enjoy the movie. Then he will make himself into a crash-test dummy. *Use the System*, Arnold has always told Heather, *or the System will use you.* Satisfied, he turns around to ask what he discovers may be the fattest man in the state, if not the entire Midwest, to please stop keeping beat to the music in the preview with his, the fattest man in the state's, sneaker on the back of his, Arnold's, seat.

WORDS TEMPORARILY FLEE Jeff Kotcheff. Cheeks chipmunked with hotdog pap, he glowers at the jewboy with the shocked indignity of a sumo wrestler whose bare foot a Pekingese has just waddled up to and shat on. Jeff stops chewing. He lowers the two-inch stub of processed meat and doughy roll and pushes his aviator glasses up on his ample nose. An ugly tomato-cream-sauce pink suffuses his ample face in the darkness. "Oh," he says in a voice that strikes Arnold as disturbingly effeminate, huge white sneaker hovering. "Oh. Sorry. Um, sorry." "No problem," replies Arnold and, smiling politely, turns back to the screen.

80

EXT. MALL OF AMERICA--DAY

CRANE SHOT: swim in slowly through an insane blizzard. South entrance of the Mall of America gradually resolves into focus. Sidewalks snowslushy below the red, white, and blue sign above the doors. Two-foot drifts piled against gigantic flowerpots and brick exterior. Whirl of dark genderless figures, hunched against the mad weather, plunging into and out of the dismal day.

81

CELAN'S THEME--a soft, sad, fluid Philip Glassian piece--rises on the soundtrack.

Camera chooses one of the bundled pedestrians and unhurriedly swoops through the entrance over his/her shoulder.

CUT TO:

INT. MALL OF AMERICA--DAY

The glittery clean tumult of commerce. In the Mall of America, weather turns out to be a dream.

No sound save for Celan's theme.

SKYCAM SHOT: the camera seems to glide through the mall's interior--over the heads of holiday shoppers; teens lapping ice-cream cones, listening to iPods; women with small kids walking and talking on cell phones as they browse the Lego Imagination Center gift shop; then up the escalators, out onto the food court balcony crammed with diners; over the edge, into space three floors above Camp Snoopy where, suspended, the camera rotates and looks back at where it came from.

FASTFORWARD: in the center of the shot, small, almost lost among the rapid sensory data, the AMC theater entrance on the fourth floor. Hold five seconds. The feeling is of a huge, shiny, Dexedrined chrome-and-glass beehive.

CUT TO:

INT. AMC THEATER NUMBER TEN--DAY

OVER-THE-SHOULDER SHOT: Celan Solen. Darkness except for the furious fuzzy white particulate light arriving from the screen like some wide rectangular stream of granulated sugar. Celan rests on his lower spine in his fastfood uniform, knees propped on the back of the seat in front of him. Patrons clustered in his vicinity. Foreground, including Celan's ear, unshaven jaw, and part of the back of his head, in focus. Background, including the movie screen itself, out of focus. It is impossible to tell, therefore, what the nebulous colorful shapes up there are doing. One has the sense of looking at a film through frosted glass.

CELAN'S THEME is step by step replaced with the massive swish of CELAN'S RESPIRATION. Wind-tunnel breathing in THX sound.

CUT TO:

INT. MOSH'S APARTMENT--DAY

MONA, Celan's cute skinny nineteen-year-old girlfriend who works at Sam Goody, is naked, standing next to an unfolded off-white futon in a meagerly furnished bedroom/living room. She holds out a pair of sexy lace panties in her right hand. Mona's skin is extraordinarily pale, breasts pert, pudendum depilated, shoe-polish black hair atop her head spiked and streaked with pink wisps. Ear, nose, and nipple piercings.

83

On the futon lies MOSH, also nineteen, skinny, naked, right knee raised bashfully to protect his privates. He looks confused. Lead guitarist for Plato's Deathmetal Tumors, an alternative Seattle band recently moved to the Twin Cities in search of a recording contract, Mosh has shaved his head and tattooed it with dark green circuitry patterns.

Mona is cheating on Celan, scamming him for money in an elaborate scheme she has devised with Mosh, with whom she is in crazy love. While both the scheme and the fact of it will become clear later on, the awareness of it should be palpable in this scene.

CUT TO:

INT. AMC THEATER NUMBER TEN--DAY

CLOSE-UP: Celan's right eye watching.

CUT TO:

INT. MOSH'S APARTMENT--DAY

Mona offering Mosh her sexy lace panties.

MONA

Don't be a dick. Come on. It'll be fun. Seriously. Do it. Come on. Do it.

MOSH

84   What? You're saying you want ...?

MONA
(Jumping up and down, little-girlish.)

Do it. DO IT. Do it do it do it. *Do it.*

CUT TO:

INT. AMC THEATER NUMBER TEN--DAY

CLOSE-UP: Celan's right eye watching.

ZOOM IN and through his right eye, into a new reality ...

CUT TO:

INT. MALL OF AMERICA: CAMP SNOOPY--DAY

SLO-MO: Kite-Eating Tree, a huge fake-bark telescoping metal pole with a huge forest-green mushroomoidal metal umbrella on top, off of which dangle scores of swing-chairs on long chains that spin scores of riders around fifty feet in the air.

ZOOM IN on one in which sits a prim SCANDINAVIAN WOMAN in her early sixties, grandchildren revolving willy-nilly around her like a flock of towheaded birds.

ZOOM IN CLOSER. Scandinavian woman's body fills the screen. She is dressed in a pastel plaid blouse and pink pants. Her seat has accidentally and uncomfortably twisted her sideways so she is looking directly into the camera lens. Her hands are palms-down on her knees. It almost appears as if she has been carved out of wood, she is so stiff. She plainly does not relish this moment in her life.

85

SLO-MO TRACKING SHOT: following her on her circular journey. Her stoic grimace. *There is a dead horse*, it seems to be saying. *There is a fence. The horse needs to be on the other side of the fence. What else can you do except pick it up, throw it over your shoulder, and begin to climb?*

ZOOM IN and through her right eye, into a new reality ...

CUT TO:

INT. CELAN'S INTERNAL ANATOMY

SPECIAL EFFECTS equivalent of SKYCAM SHOT from earlier, only instead of appearing to swim through the mall, now the camera appears to be swimming through someone's body as if on some amusement-park ride--up the taut red thread of his optic nerve; through the toboggan run of veins swirling with blood cells; into the sloshy thunderous cavern of the heart; up through the torrent of carotid artery; into the moist sparking matrix of the brain, white lightning flashing in the overcast synaptic distance.

During this voyage, CELAN'S RESPIRATION diminishes into background soundtrack. In the aural foreground:

86

CELAN (Voice Over)

Here's the really cool thing? While you can trace the origin of film all the way back to those shadows playing on the walls of Plato's cave, maybe even to the prehistoric cave paintings preceding them, contemporary cinema actually started barely a hundred years ago on December 28, 1895, in the basement of the Grand Café in Paris, when the Lumière brothers showed the first projected movies to a paying audience. Ten shorts, each about fifty seconds in length, comprised of scenes out of everyday life--a train pulling into a station, factory workers arriving at a plant, parents goofing with their kids. Initially, film embraced the Poetics of the Stage. The camera thought it was a spectator fixed in the audience watching a drama called the world.

Contemplating the act of moving somehow seemed rude. The camera thought it was nothing more than a kind of localized consciousness ...

                                                CUT TO:

INT. MOSH'S APARTMENT--DAY

Mona, still naked, is now the one lying on the unfolded futon. Mosh is on his knees between her spread legs. He is wearing her sexy lace panties. He bends forward.

CLOSE-UP: Mona's right eye watching.

ZOOM IN and through her right eye, into a new reality ...

                                                CUT TO:

INT. NINETEENTH-CENTURY PLAYHOUSE--DAY

FLICKERY, SCRATCHED, SEPIA FAUX-SONOCHROME FOOTAGE. Camera fixed in the audience. MALE ACTOR looking very much (but not quite) like Mosh and FEMALE ACTOR looking very much (but not quite) like Mona on large divan on stage in exactly the same positions Mosh and Mona have assumed in Mosh's apartment: ersatz-Mosh on his knees between ersatz-Mona's spread legs. He is wearing her sexy lace panties. He bends forward. They start kissing.

CLOSE-UP: wet eelish lingual play.

FADE TO CLOSE-UP: ersatz-Mona's right eye watching.

CELAN (Voice Over)

Only there was this problem: space in film is elastic while space in theater is rigid. They're two completely different things. Plus the basic unit of film isn't scene, but shot (with five hundred to a thousand per your standard flick), and shots can be from any number of weird angles and joined together in any number of weird combinations. You just can't do that in theater. So really what early cinematic directors discovered was theater is all about life as something relatively static, modular, linear, and by necessity over-acted. By contrast, they discovered film is all about life as permutation, nonlinearity, and nuance. The form of film is really a philosophy of disruptive movement ...

CUT TO:

INT. MOSH'S APARTMENT--DAY

CLOSE-UP of Mona's right eye watching.

CUT TO:

INT. AMC THEATER NUMBER TEN--DAY

MORPH into CLOSE-UP of Celan's right eye watching.

CELAN (Voice Over)

So I ... um ... I guess what I'm trying to say here is I sometimes sort of think of my life, basically, as a movie I can't direct ...

89

THIRTY FEET ABOVE CELAN SOLEN skitters a mouse through the warm darkness flooding the ventilation system. Tucked into the mouse's breast immediately behind its heart is the soul of Remedios the Beauty, a young woman from a small village in Colombia. When she was alive, Remedios the Beauty used to drive men mad with the sweetness of her scent, part orange, part cinnamon. Sometimes she wandered her house unclothed and sometimes she shaved her head because deciding which dress to wear or how to comb her hair seemed too much trouble. One day while hanging sheets, Remedios the Beauty began rising into the air. Her feet simply left the ground and she lifted away from earth. She became smaller and smaller until she was the size of a pearl. Then she disappeared altogether. No one ever saw her again. The chronicler who originally told her tale claimed she had ascended to heaven, but in reality she had ascended into a minute rip in the fabric of space and time that appeared that morning as an unmoving white smear of cloud in the otherwise flawless sky, and she ended up here. Remedios the Beauty will spend eternity scrambling through a lightless void that, depending on the season, is sometimes too warm and sometimes too cold, believing this is what paradise must feel like.

STUART NAVIDSON CHECKS his Palm one more time for good luck. Another email is waiting for him. *Enjoy the movie*, it says. Stuart's head jerks up. There doesn't seem to be anything out of the ordinary about the people sitting around him watching the trailers and commercials with mildly empty interest, and Stuart realizes, his veins filling with soda water, he should have told Valerie right away. He should have sat her down at the kitchen table and confessed everything. He should have told her about his stupid month-long middle-aged mistake with Brittany Laroche, the receptionist from Macalester with those wildly erotic braces. How the only thing he gained from the affair was, briefly and unrewardingly, the sensation of being minimally less old. Stuart can imagine the fight they would have had. It makes him cringe. But they would have survived. They always did, no matter what. They've been surviving for nineteen years now. Inhabiting the same life with another human being for that long is like watching yourself age in a mirror. Stuart stands, resolving here and now to phone her from the lobby. He will tell her the whole story. She will cry, naturally. She will cry, and she will shout. Stuart doesn't blame her. But he will close his eyes, shove forward, and, in the end, she will forgive him. Stuart

91

is convinced. She's *Valerie*. That's all there is to it. Stuart slips his Palm into his jacket pocket, stands, and looks around him. He sits. He feels like he is falling violently upward. He lowers his chin. He squeezes his armrests. *One thousand and one, nine hundred eighty-nine, nine hundred seventy-seven,* Stuart intones under his breath, trying to concentrate on each numeral as if it were a reason for hope, *nine hundred sixty-five, nine hundred fifty-three, nine hundred forty-one ...*

KENNETH JEHOVAH VROOMAN loves trailers because they are just like movies only shorter. He does not love the man standing up on his left and then sitting down again and beginning to count backwards under his breath with very large numbers. When something like that happens Kenneth has to think. This is related to how after the trailers Kenneth will return home without seeing the movie and microwave a creamy meatball dinner. Kenneth's older brother, Billy Aloysius Vrooman, left his body with nine hundred and thirteen other human beings in Jonestown, Guyana, on November 18, 1978. On the anniversary of that date, Kenneth buys twenty-one gerbils from different pet shops around the city and brings them home in small cardboard boxes. That's one gerbil for each year Billy was not External to His Body. Kenneth tugs on his rawhide gloves, lifts a gerbil out of its box, and applies gentle but steady pressure to its chest until its heart stops. He props the little corpses in doll chairs around a long polished mahogany doll table surrounded by polished mahogany doll chairs, raises a Dixi-cup of grape Kool-Aid in their honor, and drinks a toast. Kenneth would enjoy himself more at these celebrations if he wasn't sure he is suffering from a disease in which tattoos are spreading across his internal organs at an alarming rate. Most are based on the cabala. He knows he has to hurry to complete his lifework: writing the perfect critical study of Julia Ward Howe, the minor nineteenth-century poet who accomplished nothing of note in her ninety-one years except composing the remarkably shallow lyrics for "The Battle Hymn of the Republic" for *The Atlantic Monthly* for five dollars. Kenneth has been laboring at his lifework since February 14, 1979. He is still on chapter one.

00 : 05 : 56 : 12

SUSIE CARBONARA, THE softly plump ash-blonde in the floral-patterned blouse two seats to Ed Bergman's right, wishes she had a less pronounced tushy and that part of her nose back they removed last year because of sun damage. Ronny, her husband, is a dentist who wears Hawaiian shirts even in winter. Ronny and she have two great kids, Tyler and Taylor. Every day Susie sends God a teensy prayer of thanks. In her mind her prayers look like greeting cards with small feathery white wings. Several times a week Susie volunteers at the Presbyterian Church. Not long ago she became involved in sponsoring a cute little Nicaraguan maid named Juanita Chamorro. Juanita arrived in Minneapolis three and a half weeks ago. Until now, she has never visited a mall or seen a movie in a real movie theater, but she vacuums like an angel and her meatloaf is nummy. Susie and Ronny put her in the spare room in the basement next to Ronny's shop. It will take Susie another forty-five minutes to realize she is in the wrong movie. She wanted Juanita to see the one about the cute little Mexican maid who falls in love with the cute Manhattan billionaire who discovers he is dying of a rare blood disorder and gives away all his money. It might offer

Juanita a jim-dandy lesson about what America really stands for. Backward countries hate us, but that's only because they don't understand how we really just want to help them so they can be more like us. Even after it dawns on Susie she is in the wrong theater, she will decide to stay. You never want to show the help you can make silly mistakes. Susie Carbonara knows very few facts about the Mall of America, but she knows this one: the Chapel of Love has married more than two thousand couples since it opened in 1994. Susie thinks that is just so neat.

UNTIL NOW, JUANITA CHAMORRO has learned almost everything she knows about American culture from attending a bake sale in her honor at the Presbyterian Church and watching *Hollywood Squares* every morning while cleaning. Her favorite player is that funny black lady with those dreadlocks and teeth. "Secret Square!" Juanita Chamorro chants to herself as she dusts. "Al Roker! Al Roker! Al Roker! ... Bullfunky!" She does not know what any of these words means, but they seem to carry special significance for gringos, and so she feels it a good idea to learn them by heart. Juanita worries the family that brought her here does not smell like humans. They smell like flowers and cleaning agents. Their hair is frightening. They never raise their voices. They smile without parting their lips. Their food has no taste and their children are fat and lifeless. Juanita finds herself suspecting they might be automatons. When they go into their bedrooms at night, maybe they do not sleep. Maybe instead they plug themselves into the wall sockets and stand there with their eyes open, recharging. Once you have an idea like that in your head, it is very hard to forget. In the pocket of her new camelhair coat, Juanita carries the shrunken head

97

her great grandfather gave her as a good-luck charm the afternoon she started off down the path to catch the bus and a new life. His grandfather received it from his grandfather's grandfather who received it from Jorgre Sanjines, a Spanish explorer without a left hand, on his way back to Mexico City from a dangerous journey up the Amazon many generations ago. Juanita prays the leathery talisman will protect her spirit from the people the color of things that live under rocks.

RYAN MOODY CAN FEEL his brain cells sparkling and dying out, one by one. It is not a disagreeable sensation. After the rave began to unravel shortly past sunrise, Ryan drove over here for breakfast, a stroll, and a flick before heading back to his apartment to crash for the day. Ryan is still experiencing too much tribal tenderness to be alone just yet. Silver threads of love are filamenting over him like electric spider webs. The last glints of E winking away between his ears remind him how, on an average night, more than one hundred million pieces of interplanetary debris enter earth's atmosphere and burn up. That's what his brain cells feel like. He pictures each one flickering into a parallel universe as it expires. In infinite space even the most unlikely events transpire somewhere. That means there are infinitely many inhabited planets. That means infinitely many of them possess people with the same appearance, name, and memories as Ryan Moody. Those Ryan Moodys are experiencing every possible permutation of this Ryan Moody's life choices. When Ryan Moody's brain cells wink away on this planet, they assist in the production of other Ryan Moodys on other planets. Conversely, when the brain cells of those Ryan Moodys wink away, some of them replenish the ones this Ryan Moody is losing. It is all about the touch of skin upon skin and mathematics and the conservation of matter, believes Ryan, but mostly it is about love. Somewhere Ryan Moody is crying. Somewhere he is bending over and picking up a smooth stone by a pond on a planet whose atmosphere fizzes like pink champagne. Somewhere he has a girlfriend. Somewhere he is a girl. And somewhere Ryan Moody has already forgotten what all the other Ryan Moodys are about to think next.

00 : 05 : 59 : 01

MAX WATT IS NEARLY CERTAIN he has a blind
identical twin brother back home that suffers from
hyperhydrosis, the inability to stop sweating. Home
is a beat-up trailer in the woods on the Canadian
border. Before that, it was the backseat of his matte
olive-drab 1973 Chevy Impala, which is where Max
and Max first gave silence a leg up. The gum-
smacking salesclerk at K-Mart wouldn't let them
concentrate. All Max and Max was trying to do was
choose an electric fan to drown out the voltage of
night bugs. The girl just stood there rearranging
merchandise and making mouth sounds. The
brothers waited until after work, then bothered her
shadow. "Are we property yet?" Max's twin asked,
sweating, slamming down the trunk on their Impala.
"Buckle your mouth, honeybun," said Max. Later,
Max asked: "You think she's cured?" "She's cured,
all right," replied Max. Now Max is counting. He
has given them three colored girls down front thirty-
seven seconds to find peace within themselves or
he will invite one of them home. In back of his trailer
stands a tumbledown shed. In the floor is a trapdoor
fastened with a padlock. On the other side of the
trapdoor is a six-by-six potato cellar lined with
cinderblocks that hold in the calm. That's where

101

Josie from Wisconsin lives. Josie used to have hair the tint of din. Now she don't. Chatter is all Josie used to do, only the human tongue contains one major artery. On occasion Josie pisses herself spontaneously. After this movie Max will assemble dinner for her from dumpsters behind fastfood joints. Sometimes at breakfast Max's brother asks, staring without sight: "How long do you intend to resist me?" "Life ain't no dream, honeybun," replies Max, reaching for his box of Count Chocola. "It's a fucking *seizure*. Now give me my sugar."

DIRECTLY TO MAX WATT'S LEFT, directly behind
Trudi Chan, sits Sid Münsterberg, an undercover
cop, in row eleven, seat eight. Arms crossed, legs
stretched before him, Sid looks like a young Jerry
Garcia: upset hair, feral beard, beefy lips, aviator
glasses askew. Despite the snowstorm whirling
beyond these walls, he wears a washed-out jean
jacket and pair of scuffed-up cowboy boots.   103
Yesterday Sid received a phony tip from Ryan
Moody's ticked-off ex-girlfriend, Amanda Cocteau,
alleging Ryan is a drug dealer. On Sid's way to the
rave where Amanda told him he could find Ryan
last night, Sid stopped off at Walgreens to pick up a
prescription for some terbinafine for his toenail
fungus. The over-the-counter creams have so far
accomplished exactly diddlysquat. The yellowgreen
gunk, mildewy smell, and itchy burn are driving Sid
insane. Two days ago it spread from his right foot
to his left. Sid currently feels like a walking Petri
dish. He doesn't realize the Walgreens pharmacist,
tired, distracted, and eager to enjoy his own
Saturday evening on the town, inadvertently
confused Sid's pills with those of another customer.
A cognitive limp has entered Sid's perception. His
world seems amplified. He can hear Ryan Moody

swallowing four seats away. He can smell a mouse moving through the ventilation system thirty feet above him. He cranes back his neck and believes the screeching white projector light is the voice of Allah. With this, Sid inaugurates a new religion. It is based on the belief we do not think, but are rather thought through by the myriad fungal intelligences surrounding us. Sid Münsterberg's new religion will last just under three and a half minutes, then pass into the annals of theological arcana, having changed no one, including the founder himself.

MOIRA LOVELACE ABRUPTLY recognizes the pretty teen sitting a few seats over and down, although initially she can't quite place her. Maybe Moira passed her on her way to Dunn Brothers Coffee for a café au lait before coming here. Maybe she is a former student. Moira has a terrible time remembering former students these days. There have been oceans of them. She taught each the best she could, yet no matter what she did the stupid remained stupid, the nice nice, and their featureless faces pack a stadium in her uneasy dreams. Then it hits her: that's the one on the video Moira downloaded last week from the Face Value Productions website. What's odd is how difficult it is to place a porn star in real life. With their clothes and suburban expressions in place, they look completely unremarkable. Aside from an indistinct worn quality, this girl could pass for a college freshman. Moira recalls she had the same problem last summer when she passed Aurora Snow on a downtown street one afternoon. Later Moira learned from the newspaper that Aurora was performing at a local strip club that week. But in person she seemed like nothing more than an ordinary Midwestern teen with too much makeup on and a peculiar puffiness around the eyes, as if, somehow, too much sex leads to a kind of existential edema. Moira can't remember this girl's name, but she can't forget how good she was in the video. She played a naïve babysitter in glasses and she didn't blink or flinch. Almost everyone blinks or flinches at the end. You can't help it. But this one didn't. Her crystalline green eyes radiated composure. Remembering how they met and held the camera during the final fade, Moira Lovelace sits up a smidgen straighter in her seat, a bolt of admiration flaring through her.

SUSPENDED IN UNSUSPECTING Trudi Chan's utereus floats a two-month-old fetus filled with his mother's memories. How, on her thirty-second birthday, her husband, Carlos Metz, bought Trudi a beautiful bouquet of flowers, took her out to an elegant restaurant overlooking the San Francisco Bay, and told her he wanted a separation. Carlos said he needed to find himself. Trudi said she didn't know he was lost. Carlos said that was part of the problem. Trudi said she could help him look. Carlos said he'd like to stay married, but he needed a vacation. Just a year or so, he said. Trudi could obviously see other men, too, if she wanted. They could have an open marriage. How did that sound? Trudi thought it sounded idiotic, but she said she supposed she understood. That night Carlos slept on the futon in the guest room. At dawn, unable to sleep herself, Trudi rose and went to his bed. They made love without speaking. After breakfast, Carlos packed and left. Trudi didn't hear from him again, except in the form of divorce papers served five weeks later. Apparently he had found himself more rapidly than anticipated. Trudi decided to lose herself in her work. She arrived in Minneapolis late last night for a special meeting near the airport first thing this morning. It will be three more days before it strikes her how long it has been since her last period. Meanwhile, her fetus forgets a few of her memories every minute it moves toward birth. They peel off him like leaves peeling off an aspen in a dry autumn breeze. By the time he enters the world, he will have forgotten everything he once knew. His mind will have become a blank movie screen waiting for the man in the projection booth to reach over and flip the main switch on.

EYES SHUT, CHIN ON CHEST, Zdravko Prcac
watches himself at a party. It is difficult to tell where
the party is because the place is so poorly lit. Possibly
a basement room in Belgrade during the war. Kosa
is sitting beside him. They are happy and drinking
good vodka and laughing by candlelight with a
group of well-dressed people they have never met.
Eventually Zdravko gets up and wanders down a   109
murky hallway in search of the bar at which to refill
their drinks. He cannot find it, so he returns, makes
polite excuses, and collects his wife to go. They feel
their way up a staircase. Outside, the lights in the
city are extinguished, the streets glistening under a
full moon. Zdravko and Kosa locate their Citroën
in a nearby alley and soon Zdravko is driving. Their
house is in the countryside. It didn't used to be there,
as far as Zdravko can recall, but now it is. At the
edge of the city, they confront a police barricade.
Zdravko stops the car. Powerful flashlights blaze
into the cab. Squinting, Zdravko looks over to make
sure Kosa is all right. She is shaking. "What's
wrong?" he asks, trying to soothe her. "It's just the
police. Everything will be fine." Then Zdravko
realizes the woman sitting beside him is not his wife.
The people at the party must have stolen Kosa while

Zdravko was searching for the bar and replaced her with someone who only distantly resembles her. "I'm sorry," the woman tells him. With that, the car door swings open and four policemen claw at Zdravko, dragging him onto the hard wet road.

THERE IS NO ONE on the other end of Lakeesha
Johnson's cell-phone conversation. There never has
been. She is talking to a dead plastic mouthpiece
because she wants her friends to believe she has
friends. The reason possessing friends is so
important to Lakeesha is that possessing friends isn't
very important to her. Lakeesha's mama tells her it
isn't healthy to be happy without them, yet that is
exactly when Lakeesha feels happiest: when she is
up in her room, alone, lying on her bed, or when,
like last June, she went to the public swimming pool
all by herself and stretched out on her towel and
pretended she was on a beach white as printer paper
in Greece. Lakeesha loved the clatterchatter of other
people at a distance. How it felt like the sun was
sautéing her organs right through her skin. She
imagined the beach was one of those where nobody
wore clothes. She was there with her make-believe
boyfriend, Darius, who had hazel eyes with yellow
flecks in them and called her Baby Girl. Darius had
fallen asleep beside her. Baby Girl stood, careful not
to wake him. Without her thick glasses, experience
arrived as a pastel smear. She shuffled into the surf
and buoyed there, unaware of the muscular current
nudging her south. Before long, she felt lighter,

111

breezier. When she stepped onto the beach again, she discovered she was lost among an overgrown garden of blurred bodies. She stood several minutes, trying to focus on all that smudged nakedness. Then she sucked up her self-esteem and launched north, bending at the waist here, cupping her hands on her kneecaps there, examining the abundance of jointless thumbs reposing among dense curls in search of the one that would signal Darius's presence. Pulling herself back from that reverie, she discovered she was no longer lying on her towel by the public swimming pool. She was lying instead on the bottom of it, wafting like a heavy jellyfish. Lakeesha had already taken her first breath of water. She didn't think it would be as bad as everyone said it would be, but it was worse, and so she tried to pinpoint tranquility inside her. It was there and it was gone and it was there and it was gone and then her world erupted into foam and splashes and terrified shouts. A school of angry hands attacked her, grabbing at her, towing her, yanking her gorgeous black sea-anemone hair. Next she was lying on her left side on coarse concrete, being unsightly. Her sinuses and throat felt as if she had inhaled gasoline and lit a match. People were telling her things, but Lakeesha just lay there, refusing to open her eyes, refusing to listen to what they were saying, thinking very hard about not thinking and taking some pleasure in the stingy impossibility of it again and again.

KATE FRAZEY HAS LOST HER BATTLE. She did
what she could, but she has already been asleep
seven seconds. In that time, she has been visited by
three dreams. In the first, she stood watching the
Sirens on a rocky gray beach littered with their
victims' bones. Perched among the branches of
leafless trees, the Sirens lamented their clawed
hands, vestigial wings, and sterile wombs. No matter
how they tried, they were unable to prevent their
lamentations from sounding outrageously beautiful.
In the second, two men in business suits tenderly
strapped Kate face down into a large elaborate
medieval torture device resembling a loom. To be
released, all Kate had to do was articulate her
offenses. The problem was she couldn't recollect
with any clarity what those offenses might have
been. As a dermal prompt, the torture-loom was
busy etching them into her bloody bare back, upside
down and reversed, in a language reminiscent of
Arabic that Kate could not read even if she had been
able to see it. In the dream she presently occupies,
she is sprinting down lightless tunnel after tunnel
in what she fears may be an infinite aluminum
burrow. The Holy Spirit's breath deafens her as she
pushes forward. Exhausted, she does not believe

113

she can go much farther. Little by little, the idea begins to coalesce inside her she is not a human being any more. She may be a mole. She may be a mouse. Something may or may not be chasing her. Something may or may not be catching up. And this, for better or worse, will be her life. Kate Frazey tries to force herself awake, but fails repeatedly. She tries to change the course of her dream, but it just keeps pouring in at her. Kate Frazey just keeps sprinting.

LILY GRODAL WAS VACUUMING her living room carpet in her milky blue jogging suit and sneakers, frizzled bronze hair held partially in check by a tortoise-shell barrette, when she decided poop on this, she was going to a movie. It was Charlie's weekend with the kids and she wasn't going to waste it. She left the upright standing where it was, strode into the kitchen, tugged on her parka, swept her car keys and wallet into her pocket, and hustled out the back door into the furious snow. Her plan was to ask the person in the ticket booth what the very next film showing was and see that one. She would be home in plenty of time to finish vacuuming, take a nice hot bubble bath, and order in a large pepperoni pizza before Charlie dropped off the kids around seven. Danny is six, Russ eight, and Lily, who loves them both frantically, wishes several times a day she had had girls. The moment she entered theater ten she almost broke her neck stumbling over some poor guy's crutches sticking into the aisle. She dropped her box of Dots. When she tried to apologize to the man with the crutches, some creepy sweaty guy one row back hissed at her. To avoid him, Lily felt her way down front, cut across the sticky no-man's land between the first row and the screen, and took the

115

only empty seat she could confirm was in truth empty in the sputtering lightdark. It is seat one, row four. Settling, she tugs off her parka, bunches it against her abdomen, and, quietly as possible, starts peeling open her box of candy. Slipping a lemon gumdrop into her mouth, Lily Grodal hears a woman's southern-twanged voice behind her ask in a loud, matter-of-fact voice, as if it were asking about the weather: "So you think them spacemen is gonna send us another sign soon, Johnny Ray, er *whut*?"

TIMES IN HIS LIFE Lewis Smoodin chose the fifth seat in the fifth row for his viewing pleasure: 1. Times he believed it must be a beautiful day outside, only not in the city where he currently resided: 895. Times he delighted that English, with its vocabulary of over 1,000,000 words (3x more than French), is the largest language in history: 21. Times he hoped the invention of the iPod would transform his life into a musical: 479. Times he was forced to stop eating the meal he was eating because one kind of food on his plate made contact with another kind: 1,833. Times in his life Lewis liked being touched by another human being: 7. Times in the last month he ate at the Mall of America food court: 37. Times he has been able to tell with certainty if someone were interested or bored by what he was saying: 3. Times someone said something to Lewis Smoodin for which he had no reply: 1,376. Times married: 1. Times he began a conversation in the Mall of America food court with an unfamiliar person by saying *My age is forty-three and I am five-feet-six-inches tall when I don't wear my shoes*: 112. Times Lewis employed the term *foveated vision* in the public sphere to denote how the human eye can only focus on one very small area at any given moment: 1.

117

Times divorced: 1. Times he forgot he had a brother fighting in Iraq: 1,082. Times in his life he employed the term *saccadic movement* in the public sphere to denote how the human eye, in order to compensate for the aforementioned foveated vision, reflexively moves every 1/20 of a second in an attempt to perceive the entirety of its surroundings: 5. Times his brother fighting in Iraq forgot to acknowledge Lewis's birthday: 43. Times he has had a birthday to forget: 43. Times Lewis Smoodin wished time could run backward: 4,502.

FRED QUOCK'S wandering thoughts stray down a passageway from his childhood. The pinkie of a smile widens beneath his vestigial salt-and-pepper mustache. A lively blue autumn afternoon on the other side of his sister Leni's bedroom window. Downstairs, his mother cooking supper. Onions. Meatloaf. Mushrooms. Fred is five, Leni eleven, and Leni has just decked him out in one of her favorite Easter dresses. He looks exactly like a princess on her way to a ball, Leni tells him, and Fred feels instantly pretty. Their father, Fred Quock, Sr., a cardiologist at Sacred Heart in Eugene, brings home 45's from the office once a month as inexpensive presents for his kids. The 45's are anthologies of irregular heart rhythms meant to teach doctors the sounds of disease. Leni and Fred listen to them on Leni's black plastic RCA stereo with the volume turned way up. Fred raises his little arms and makes little fists of his little hands and squats and swivels on his little hips to the organic beat. He would be happy if he could know this blue moment would dilate and dilate and go on dilating forever. Whenever Fred daydreams lately, this is the vivid room to which he returns. The comforting smell of his mother's cooking. The lacy crinkle of his new

119

dress in his fingers. The way his sister Leni never takes her chocolate eyes off him because he is not a chubby boy with a big nose and buckteeth that Randy Roberts from up the block wedgies. No. He is Fred Quock the princess and Fred Quock the princess is the stuffed animals huddling on his sister's pillows, the gusty sunlight, the way this autumn afternoon brightly arranges itself. Fred Quock is the Frug. The Twist. He is the Funky Chicken.

KOSA PRCAC'S GHOST WAVERS like a strand of nearly invisible seaweed several millimeters to the right of her husband's wheelchair. Each time she attempts touching him, her fingers pass through his face and the couple experiences another recollection from their years together. When she was young, Kosa always felt the need to apologize to anyone she met for anything she did. That changed the evening she met Zdravko at the opera. She was nineteen, he twenty-seven, and Zdravko was wearing his handsome military dress uniform. When he bowed to kiss her hand, Kosa knew she would marry him someday. Six weeks later, they took a drive in the countryside. Zdravko was behind the wheel, the convertible's top down. Grassy hills rose and ducked around them in a silver haze of sunshine. They stopped by a wooden gate and carried their wicker picnic basket out to a big willow standing alone in a deserted pasture. After drinking too much wine, they began to kiss. Soon they were helping each other undress. Beneath Zdravko's slacks, Kosa discovered a frilly pair of women's undergarments. Beneath Kosa's slip, Zdravko discovered an underdeveloped penis and half-formed female parts. They made delicious

121

exploratory love for hours. Fingers passing through her husband's face again, Kosa recalls the evening in Belgrade she turned sixty-four and treated herself by visiting a soothsayer. After studying Kosa's palm for many minutes, the ancient woman told Kosa she had no future. Kosa looked up, startled. "I'm sorry, sweetheart," the soothsayer said, "but you've already been dead three years." Appalled at the woman's insolence, Kosa rose and left without paying.

NADI SLONE, ONE SEAT IN FRONT of Claude
Méliès and two behind Jeff Kotcheff, is recalling the
pub drama she saw in London last month. Nadi
was there for the opening of her first exhibition
outside the U.S. Her work consists of traveling to
famous museums and taking clandestine
photographs of people passing by famous pieces of
art without seeming to notice them--daydreaming,   123
chatting, tending to their astronaut infants in baby
carriages--without, however, ever documenting the
famous piece of art itself. The evening before her
flight back to America she had nothing to do, so Nadi
picked up a *Time Out,* checked the fringe listings,
and chose a performance of Peter Handke's *My Foot,
My Tutor* playing upstairs in a small pub not far from
the Elephant & Castle tube stop. The performance
space was no larger than a bedroom. Admission was
six pounds fifty. There were two actors and three
audience members, including Nadi. There were two
rows of seats, each comprised of four folding chairs.
If you stuck your legs out, you would trip the
players. Yet they never broke stride, never dropped
their personae, displayed nothing save intense
industry and surprising talent. Afterward, they took
their bows with professional deadpan faces. The

three audience members, including Nadi, clapped fervently. One, a distinguished elderly gentleman who might have been a banker, judiciously rose to his feet to provide the actors with a standing ovation. That night, back at her B&B, Nadi dreamed everyone everywhere in London stopped where they were at the stroke of noon one Monday and began singing the same exquisite aria. Three minutes later, they ceased simultaneously and went on with their lives just like before. The Incident, at it came to be known, was never repeated.

00 : 06 : 42 : 16

THE ONE WITH THE CELL PHONE: she's the one who will date Max's blind twin brother. Max wonders if Max will be able to tell she is colored. Maybe the smell. Max considered inviting home the disgusting pig who just tripped in the aisle instead, but feels Josie from Wisconsin would prefer someone closer to her own age. They will have more in common to be silent about. The inner ear, Max remembers, consists of a cochlea, semicircular canals, and auditory nerve. The cochlea and semicircular canals are filled with a water-like fluid. In part this is due to the fact that sometimes it is hard to chase down sleep. Max hasn't had none in two days. "Are we having thoughts again?" his twin brother, sweating, asked him while staring sightlessly at the unplugged TV with the bashed-in screen last night in the trailer. "Put a sock in it, honeybun," said Max, sitting beside him. Not long after that, Max rose without a word, tramped out to the Impala through the rising blizzard, and began the long drive south with the radio off. In his trunk, he carries a burlap sack. This is for the food from the dumpsters. In his coat pocket, he carries a vial of hush tonic, a handkerchief, and a small Phillips screwdriver. "The two of us makes three," he will

125

whisper into the colored girl's ear as he helps her locate the peace within herself. Maybe this will take place in an unlit corner of a parking garage, maybe in an empty ladies room behind a gas station. "Am I alone yet, cupcake?" Max will whisper into her ear. "Am I alone?"

00 : 06 : 44 : 02

VITO PALUSO IMAGINES each brief shot in the experimental short he is making a heavy gray stone. His project will be to sew them all together into a suit of rocks, which he will wear everywhere he goes. Some people will say the suit makes walking a formidable task, but Vito Paluso believes it will also allow him to fully appreciate each step he takes. He plans to embroider it with delicate butterfly wings.   127

THE SECOND MIGUEL GONZALEZ touches her down there, Angelica Encinas understands she does not like boys. Boys make noise. They breathe like old people sleeping. Their muscles feel all wrong and sometimes they smell like iron filings and this is not desire. There are many other words for what this is but *desire* is not one of them. Angelica likes Miguel's short spiky hair. It reminds her of a styling brush with nylon pins. She likes the dimple that forms to the left of his mouth but not to the right when he grins. But Miguel is a boy and boys say nothing for half an hour and when they finally do say something it is clear they don't really want to be saying it. Angelica withdraws her hand from the hot bowed thing inside his fly and understands she does not like boys. Maybe it is just that she does not like this one. Maybe that is it. Only she does not really believe what she is thinking. She is just trying on the idea like a new pair of pre-washed jeans to see if they fit her hips. Angelica withdraws her hand and reaches down and pushes Miguel's away from her chocho beneath her panties beneath her dress. She sits up straight and begins paying too much attention to the previews although really she is not paying any attention to them at all. Because girls.

128

Because their skin. Because the way they touch each other. Angelica wonders what this person who just put his fingertip into her chocho will do next. What he will say or not say. Angelica wonders what it is she is trying to feel. Because it is not Miguel Gonzalez sitting next to her anymore. This much is clear. It is not him. It is a staticky wedge of disbelief and resentment. It is just another boy.

STUART NAVIDSON IS RIGHT. Someone really is tailing him: the athletic man in the Armani suit and designer stubble sitting two rows behind him whose name is Giuseppe Rosi. Giuseppe Rosi has made a mistake. His job is convincing people whom he doesn't know that they don't want what they think they want. Once or twice a month he receives a phone call, drives to the address given him, and starts improvising. Unluckily, when the last one arrived, he was in the middle of a great bench press at the Los Campeones Fitness Center. Giuseppe set the bar back in its cradle, picked up his cellular, listened, and repeated the information the man on the other end told him without actually writing it down. Then he got back to his set. In the time it took him to complete seven more presses, his memory had transposed two digits in the mark's address. Giuseppe therefore should not be convincing Stuart Navidson, whom he can hear counting backwards anxiously two rows in front of him, that he doesn't want what he thinks he wants, but another man of similar build and attributes who happens to live one block north of Stuart in a much nicer neighborhood. Giuseppe reaches into the inner pocket of his Armani jacket and fishes for his own

Palm device in order to send Stuart a message asking him to please shut the fuck up. People are trying to watch a fucking movie here.

AT THE PRESBYTERIAN church bake sale, tall white-haired women in pastel suits surrounded Juanita Chamorro like chickens waiting for feed. All Juanita wanted to do was eat the slice of apple pie topped with a huge dollop of whipped cream they had offered her. **The bus she was riding toward her new life stopped late the first night on a winding road high in the mountains. The full moon was very bright.** Juanita calculated a long time, carefully constructed a gringo sentence of thanks, and stumblingly articulated it. The tall white-haired women in pastel suits unleashed a verbal hurricane in response. **There had been an accident.** When it became clear to them Juanita had no idea what they were saying, they spoke louder, not slower. **There was no railing and the bus in front of hers had gone over the side of the cliff.** Juanita was wearing her best cotton dress, white decorated with yellow, blue, and red flowers. Her mother had made it for her. Every night Juanita washed it, sorry it smelled less and less like the memory of her village. **From what Juanita could see from her seat, it appeared as if someone had stepped on a large milk carton far below among the rocks.** They made her stand on a stage while she worked at her apple

132

pie, saying things about her she didn't understand. **Around the large crushed milk carton were scattered what looked like fingertips dressed in skirts and slacks and scarves.** They began to applaud her at the second she slipped the last piece of apple pie into her mouth. Someone put a microphone into her hand and Juanita dropped it. It made a squeal when it hit the floor. **One of the fingertips, Juanita could see, was still moving. It was trying to crawl away from the bus. The old man beside her was still sleeping. The driver of her bus was standing outside with several other people, pointing and watching.** Juanita couldn't think of anything to say. Everyone waited politely. "America," Juanita began, and then her mind went blank. "America," she began again, then paused. **She remembered how the fingertip appeared to be trying to use its arms to swim among the boulders.** "America," she said into the microphone, "is a land of excellent pies." Then she handed the microphone back. **Soon the fingertip stopped trying to use its arms to swim.** The tall white-haired women in pastel suits erupted into charmed applause. They loved Juanita, no matter what she said or did. **The fingertip lay its head down on the ground very gently and then there was no more movement.** The one who had handed Juanita the microphone locked her in a powerful hug, kissing the air next to her right ear, then kissing the air next to her left. **Juanita waited for what would happen next, but nothing did.**

1. A MINOR TINGLING IN HER FINGERTIPS. Cynthia Morgenstern looks down. They are gone. She looks down. They are not gone. Cynthia is almost positive she is gradually becoming transparent.

2. When she was a teenager she took a trip to L.A. to see a taping of her favorite women's talk show, *My Feelings*. A bloated man stood behind the camera waving a white towel over his head to indicate when the audience was supposed to clap. During a break he yelled at her because she kept looking at the monitors to see how she was doing. "You're not *watching* television, lady," the bloated man said testily. "You're *making* it."

3. If Cary Grant ran a hand through his beautiful hair, she is convinced, beautiful dreams would pour out.

4. When the theater within the theater is gone, you get to return home. Sometimes this takes a minute. Sometimes this takes a lifetime.

5. Fade in.

6. Fade out.

134

JUST HERSELF ON YOUR FINGERTIP, just like
that, just the way it slid in, the astonishing slick heat
of inside her, just these things, just her tiny palm
around you, the way it felt a little like pain too, just
you breathing, just the seriousness of it, just the way
your fingertip slid into her and then everything
splintered, just the way she suddenly shoved you
back down inside your pants, just like some stupid
rolled-up sock she found in a drawer, just the way
she turned away from you, just you sitting there
asking with your eyes what the hell she did that for,
just her wanting to see what it felt like to tease you,
just so she could tell all her friends about it
tomorrow, just so they could all laugh at you behind
your back, just her thinking she could do it one
minute and not the next like it was some kind of
joke, just being mean just to see if she could, just her
letting it happen but then letting it not happen, just
the leaky sting of it like you have to pee real bad but
can't, just you sitting here feeling so dumb, just her
sitting beside you being so like whatever, just you
breathing, just her being that harsh, just like you are
nothing, just like that.

00 : 07 : 34 : 03

LISTENING TO THE TEENAGE COUPLE going at it behind her changes Trudi Chan's mind. She finds herself restless and doesn't feel like seeing a movie anymore. Gathering her coat, she rises to leave. Her analysis of malls has revealed a subculture almost no one knows about: a singles scene with its own meeting places, secret handshakes, and coded phrases. Trudi hasn't had sex since Carlos left. This afternoon will be different, fresh, open to chance. She will order a pink drink at Gators and wipe the hard drive called Trudi Chan. For the next two hours her name will be Mary Sapphire. As Mary steps past Vito Paluso into the aisle, the fetus suspended in her uterus experiences an intense sensation of the color red.

136

SOMETIMES EXPLORING, FINGERING small tubes of alphahydroxy cream or a floss dispenser on a bathroom shelf, Anderson feels compelled to evacuate his bowels. The muscular excitement augments inside him, distant at first, then nearer, a part of him, and then he has to go. He unbuckles his belt, unzips his fly, lowers his beige LL Beans down around his ankles, and lowers himself onto his neighbor's toilet. If there is a magazine rack 137 nearby, he enjoys thumbing through articles in *People* and *Newsweek*. Every so often, though, sitting there, a picture comes to him of himself sitting there, minding his own business, when, a genetic unfortunate, one of his carotids blows at the liberating rush. Then the family whose house he is investigating returns home from their daughter's piano lesson or trip to the supermarket to find their neighbor lying on their bathroom floor in a pool of his own shit and blood. Like the fallen King. Like Elvis himself, with those pills and fried-peanut-butter-and-banana sandwiches strewn around him. Anderson cannot conceive of a sight more completely hideous. Wiping, he shakes clear his head. Standing, he hoists his pants, zips his fly, buckles his belt. He washes his hands at the sink shaped like a caricature of a shell. He uses the lilac-scented soap shaped like the caricature of a flower, twice, then strolls down the hallway, through the kitchen, and out the back door, leaving the toilet unflushed, a commanding trace of himself in his wake.

00 : 07 : 55 : 11

NO, MAX WATT tells himself as that chink girl gets to her feet right in front of him, her world of commotion blocking his view: *No, her.*

139

NADI SLONE FEELS SOMETHING brush against her calves and believes it might be death itself. She shivers involuntarily. Then the sensation has vanished and Nadi forgotten it. While the stray cat passes beneath her seat, two strangers in top hats and frock coats escort Kate Frazey to a quarry on a stark, full-moon night lit by a German Expressionist filmmaker. Tomorrow is Kate's thirty-first birthday. Reaching an unexceptional spot along the packed-dirt road, the strangers stop and ask her to kneel. Kate does. One reaches out and holds her throat. The other produces a knife and stabs her in the heart deferrentially. He rotates the blade twice, clearing his windpipe with small, uneasy coughs as he works.

140

ATHENA FULAY, THE thin old woman swaddled in a whirlwind of black shawls, diamond brooches, and whitepink pearl necklaces two seats to the left of Ed Bergman in row four, has been alive since 1731. Athena once accompanied Blake's patron, Thomas Butts, to the poet's summerhouse in south London for lunch and discovered William and Catherine reading *Paradise Lost* aloud to each other in the garden, naked. "Come in!" Blake cried. "It's only Adam and Eve, you know!" They did. When she left, Athena was more or less immortal. She met Peter Quinn, Bloomington's first white settler, shortly after he arrived in America in 1843, formed part of the first audience watching those eight brief moviettes in the basement of the Grand Café in Paris on December 28, 1895, and shared tea with an elderly Julia Ward Howe in her Boston home one afternoon at the turn of the century. Athena found Howe insufferable. God this, God that, loving, loving, loving. Many of the living dead find immortality as sad and tedious as Athena found Howe, but Athena is not among them. For her, as for Blake and Catherine, change turns trees into fountains of light, people's faces into incandescent masks. Everything in her world is beewing buzz. Existence for Athena is like a good novel by Mr. Charles Dickens: she has

141

to keep reading, keep turning the pages, although she knows the ending will always somehow disappoint, that after the last period on the last sentence on the last page there will always be nothing but book cover, and then nothing but nothing. Athena's ambition is to invite as many people as possible along with her into her almost-forever party while she can. She leans forward and parts her lips to invite another.

00 : 08 : 16 : 01

LARA MCLUHAN CLOSES HER EYES and is sitting on a bench at Nine West, tugging on that adorable pair of mod boots with the white stripes made of plastic at the top she noticed yesterday, surrounded by naked old men with droopy buttocks and hairy backs beating off, while, four rows behind and three to her left, Celan Solen tries to figure out why reality feels so inadequate simply because you can't look at it through a frame like you can a movie.

SHORTLY AFTER HIS RETURN from Vietnam in
1969, a buddy of his turned Rex Wigglie onto the
perfect scam. Rex hired himself out as a professional
vampire hunter. He would arrive on the scene late
at night, produce a crucifix and ash-wood stake, and
tell his clients to vacate the premises. Then he would
unroll his sleeping bag, get a good night's sleep, and
144 in the morning pronounce the surroundings safe.
Now Rex feels two quick pricks on the back of his
neck, reaches up to brush them away, and locates
nothing but air. In two weeks, his eyes filling with
blood instead of tears after stubbing his toe on a
doorjamb, Rex will fetch up, shocked, unable to
absorb the coarse revelation about his new state of
being. The last time Rex had sex was on April 30,
1975, the day Saigon fell. He doesn't really remember
it, except that the girl was a holy roller from Lockjaw,
Idaho, who obtained most of her notions about truth
from country-western ballads, to which she
introduced Rex. That's when he learned there are
more interesting things than having sex. Since then,
he has composed 4,312 lyrics, all concerning animals,
mostly falcons and fish, although frogs have also
put in sporadic appearances, and how nature is not
nice, except sometimes, when it is. Try as he might,

Rex can't think of anything else to write about, even though he lives in a split level in the suburbs and secretly feels he has seen enough nature out his kitchen window to last him centuries. Absentmindedly rubbing the back of his neck, he experiences an apparition: the Mall of America swarmed with thousands of Rex Wigglies, puffy eyed, pale faced, jelly bellied, arms reaching before them robotically as they shuffle-stumble forward on a zombie shopping spree. Rex Wigglie blinks to make the vision go away, and it does, but only for a second.

PATTING THE POCKET of his Army-surplus jacket, Max Watt gets up and begins ambulating sideways toward the aisle, a human crab, while Anderson Bates questions why more people aren't bothered by the idea that in excess of ninety percent of all household dust is comprised of sloughed-off skin cells: we are all, he frets, literally busy raining ourselves away.

LILY GRODAL floats in a hot fragrant bubble bath, submerged up to her chin. She feels sleepy and tingly. Her children do not exist. She has never met her husband Charlie. Lily doesn't know what she is looking for in her life, but it wasn't any of that. She wants to be somebody else, but this evening Lily will settle for being herself. A single red rose leans in a green glass vase at the far end of the tub. She reaches down for the washcloth between her legs with the fuzzy notion of unfolding it across her face, and her elbow by chance knocks into the hairdryer on the stool beside her. Before Lily can respond, the hairdryer splashes into the sudsy water in a silverwhite flash of sparks and smoke and ... and, hey, someone has fallen down over there. Someone has fallen down in the aisle. Lily turns to see what has happened. It is that creepy guy who hissed at her. He isn't getting up. Everyone is staring in his direction. Serves him right, she thinks, an arc of guilty alarm for entertaining such an ugly thought bounding through her.

147

00 : 08 : 34 : 12

TRUDI CHAN PUSHES THROUGH the door at the back of the theater and breaches into light so smartingly concentrated it makes her immediately squinch shut her eyes. She swerves and stops and steadies herself, then presses on for the exit.

A HEAVY THUMP. Zdravko Prcac recoils from his half-sleep. In front of him is a young woman in a drab steelblue apron and headscarf, twenty or twenty-one, mopping the floor of a yellow-tiled interrogation cell at the Omarska camp, the linoleum floor tiles spattered with teeth and chunks of bloody hair. She is living inside her own rhythms, unaffected by her profession. 149

KOSA PRCAC'S GHOST darts left, into and out of her husband's mind, the passing impression being one of flying extremely fast through a silver haze of sunshine.

00 : 08 : 35 : 06

ANGELICA ENCINAS'S hand leaps out in search
of Miguel Gonzalez's.

151

00 : 08 : 35 : 06

MIGUEL GONZALEZ'S hand pushes Angelica
Encinas's away.

00 : 08 : 35 : 06

RIBCAGE THROBBING, the stray cat dashes back into the insanity of legs.

MAX WATT DOESN'T KNOW he is taking a tumble until the left side of his face hammers the carpet. Then Max and Max are walking with their father through spindly woods behind their beat-up trailer in northern California. Max is eight and Max is eight. It is raining lightly. Max hopes the opal droplets will help explain the world to him. Their father, a bison in overalls, is carrying his whipping belt in one hand and holding the brothers' wrists in the other. He is going to make them do a couple of things. After awhile, they pause by a dead gray tree. His father tells Max and Max to drop their drawers. "We ain't nobody's children," he announces, lifting his belt over his head. Max and Max barter looks. "I don't want to, daddy," Max says. "It don't matter none, boys," his father says, lifting, "it's just the way things is. First you get born. Then you get whomped. Then you get whomped some more." Next Max is up on his knees in the theater again, everybody using their eyes against him, and then he is scramble-limping up the aisle, through the door into the lobby, and she is nowhere, nowhere at all, and Max Watt is everywhere but here.

154

00 : 08 : 45 : 21

BETSI BLISS recites a little prayer to herself for that poor man who tripped and hopes he didn't hurt himself too bad. That kind of thing happens to everybody. Nothing to be ashamed of. It's just the Lord's reminder to us all that we're not quite as special as we sometimes think we are. Then Betsi Bliss's back begins itching. Everything around her distends weakly, a few millimeters, and contracts again.

155

00 : 08 : 49 : 11

SOMETIMES THEY FEEL RUBBERY when they bump into your cheek, Lara McLuhan thinks, just like wet handballs.

VLADISLAV DOVZHENKO lunges and twists against the Shock Troops console in back of the arcade on the fourth floor. Lights strobe. Subwoofer explosions rumble. Each time he gets a kill, Vladislav can feel the electronics vibrating beneath his groin. Now he's got an erection. He is already on level seven, deep into the enemy stronghold, some sort of dark, shadow-hectic, film-noir factory complex, bolts the size of bodies, gears the size of cars, metal catwalks crisscrossed over vats of black tinfoil fluid, and he can sense those baby mamas by the skeet-shooting game admiring his moves, and now he's got an erection. They are American girls with long blond hair like California and David Lee Roth and they are wearing tight torn jeans and black leather jackets and they think Vladislav is a total stud. When he rolls a million, he makes up his mind, he will stroll over and introduce himself, chat them up a little, suggest they head down to the food court for a burger and fries together. They can't be more than fifteen. How hot is that? But Vladislav has to concentrate. This is no time to let his attention drift. This is no time to mess up a good thing.

ARTIFICIAL WHITES AND BLUES sputter over
Byron Metnick's face as on the screen automatic
assault weapons clatter, tanks burst over barricades,
and buildings implode in columns of dust and
raining debris. From what Byron can tell, he is not
just watching trailers for a war movie, but trailers
for the sequel or prequel to a war movie, though he
158 can't figure out what war it is supposed to be, doesn't
think he saw the original version, and doesn't in any
case much care. He is still occupied with being
impressed by how utterly that guy wiped out in the
opposite aisle. Byron contemplates following him
from the theater just to make sure he's okay, but
something on the screen tugs back his attention. The
soldier's face there in the background. Six GI's are
huddled in a bomb crater surrounded by ragged
structures that might once have been an apartment
block, bullets searing overhead, mortars slamming
down around them. The faces of the five in the
foreground are sweaty, warped with forebodings of
doom. But the sixth one, the one belonging to the
guy in the background, appears almost relaxed.
Although he exists faintly out of focus, Byron
determines he is not so much huddling as reclining
on the sandy embankment, and he's got something

in his hands. Cards. He's shuffling a deck of cards, playing what seems to be a game of solitaire with himself. And his face is familiar. *Very* familiar. It hits Byron precipitately he is looking at himself up there. "Hey," he says to nobody, scanning the theater for corroboration and support, heart punching around blindly inside his chest. "Hey ... um ... hey ..."

BLINDFOLDED, MOIRA LOVELACE sprawls across a bare mattress, wrists and ankles tied to the bedposts by strips of torn pillowcase. The video camera's black eye at the foot of the bed stares at her from its tripod. Three football players in gold and midnight-blue uniforms form a semi-circle on the far side. "We gonna teach you how to be a nice girl, Miss Lovelace," says the first. "You wanna do that? Teacher wanna learn what a nice girl is?" Helmets tucked beneath arms, they check her out with ominous wonder. Then the reality of the situation edges up on the second player. "Yo," he says. "Yo. Wait up. What the fuck are we *doing* here, guys?" "Don't be a pussy, pussy," says the third. His face slides into a smile. "I mean, jeez, Bobby. We just having a little fun, man, you know? Chill out. Bitch wants a lesson. We gonna give her a lesson. Ain't that right, Miss Lovelace?" Moira's wrists burn. She closes her eyes beneath her blindfolds and conjugates. "Cupio, cupis, cupit," she says. "Cupimus, cupitis, cupiunt." "Cupio, cupis, cupit," the football players respond in unison. "Cupimus, cupitis, cupiunt."

160

… BUT, LEON MOPATI CONSIDERS, picture this: rather than angels, a great conspiracy behind our backs. That corpulent man slurping. That skinny usher talking to himself. That unlucky fellow falling in the aisle. Got up. Good. Made it. Sometimes the best revenge being simply to survive. Another premise: everyone who touches one of their unsteady lives has been paid to act her or his part. Why not? Disprove it. Go on. Let us call it religion. Well, you say, well: just ask them. Only don't you see? The cinerati maintain all film history boils down to the not-so-short distance between the Lumière Brothers and Méliès. Realism, documentary, mimesis: magic, vision, spectacle. Choose your side and take your Rorschach. Whatever they tell you, whether they affirm or deny it, is part of the script the fallen fellow's not privy to, or the fat one, or the skinny. What did they used to? *Photoplay.* That's it. Lovely language from the days when language was thought. *Frolicking light.* Film as architecture in motion. A luminous building that walks around you. Sneak up on them when they're not. That's the spirit. Hide in a closet. Shinny beneath a bed. Wait for them to speak when they think you're not around waiting for them to speak. Adrift. In the brightness.

161

What a terrible place to. The hot white day. Whiff of baked. But where is she now, my beekeeper? Saada sitting. Saada strolling. Saada shopping store to store. What is she thinking as I think *What is she thinking?* Sipping coffee in Dunn Brothers. Reaching for a bra in Victoria's Secrets. Don't you see? That's merely part of the same script that affirms you're hiding in the closet or beneath the bed. Okay: then Ockham's razor, you say. Principle of parsimony. Plurality not to be assumed without und so weiter. Ciao. There goes God again, lugging His valise behind Him. Yahweh thumbing His way down the autobahn. Auf Weiderretten. Shalom. Don't forget to. Right. Our sense of these things changing as they change because we begin life as one person and end it as many. Like that artist who did paintings of strangers, then called them all self-portraits. Except isn't it. What? Except isn't it more parsimonious to assume everyone is working off a script he doesn't have access to than it is every man, woman, and child is running willy-nilly and topsy-turvy through a pluriverse, scriptless? Homeless. Scylla and. Wait. Nausicaa on the waterfront-what was her name? That book being, I mean. Her. Yes. Daisy. Daisy Buchanan. That's it. West Egg, yolk of his story. I'll always be Nick at heart, odd man out, Nick at night who wears his mind on his sleeve. He is sometimes happy just being older. Love among the ruins. The olive trees. The disintegration of a certain afternoon. Let us call it going to the movies. The silverscreen dock. Green residence of the head. Born Gatz, wasn't he? Changing as we. The opposite being the opposite of breathing. Because it is such a public medium, celluloid, continuously about how we live together continuously. Like architecture that way, too. What we think, in other words, isn't what we see. These difficult objects of the imagination, these angels continuing their laughs, lightmist issuing from their mouths. We are so nice to each other because our religions are not. What a strange. Why can't we learn to live in pieces with each other? Is it therefore a coincidence that every person whose skull has been opened has had a brain inside it? Think. The opposite being the opposite. All other skulls are stuffed with. What? Not straw, say, but slategray snails. Our idea of the Paraclete. Why not? Prove me wrong. Go ahead. Please. No, really. Try. Because in this place lightmist is no angel's breath but a clamor from morning to midnight. A filmic racket crazying the afternoon. Mouths breaking down popcorn. Milk Duds. Runts. Rasinets. Hot Tamales. Sweetarts. Gobstoppers. (What a word!) Almond Joy. Yes. Hosanna to the Mercurial Age. A-chew. Bless you. Sniffle. Merci. Those teens down front talking to the screen as if with twenty-foot friends. Childish Americans with their eyes shut against the. World. All they want is more. Hear no evil, see no. What do you suppose that sound ...? Cellophane rip of candybox wrapping. Where did the kissing? The nothing that is not there and. Life Savers. Pack your own, rowing through the changing minutes homeward. Nice. A sermon there. And so back to faithful Saada. Here we are again. Nevertheless open up the head of someone you claim has jewelry in it, you say, and all you will find is another brain domiciled within. Sure. Of course. That's easy for you to say. Proves my point. Once a skull is popped, chances are you will locate a brain in it. Tell me something I don't know. Tell me, for example, how we touched hands purely because touching hands seemed the right thing to do. On that gravelly path. She loved me then. But does she love me now, picking through the sales rack at Casual Corner? Next to love stands the desire for it. When you're young, you confuse the one with the other. Middling into age, you confuse desire and love with affection and reliability. Who would want it otherwise? And so if she sat next to me now, a stranger, would she care? Or would she merely watch the feature before her, our elbows unintentionally untouching, then rise and drift off to shop some more with someone more? The idea so fragile. Too immediate for any speech. Isn't that. What? Sad. Yes. Yes, it is. Very. A moving picture. Changing as I. The opposite being the same, in some sense, too. Ditto with an x-ray. Thermogram. CAT-scan. Yet the next person whose head you crack open might just have a cranium stuffed with honey-scented blossoms, violets and camellias, mayflowers and monkhoods, snowberries and zinnias. In any case, that's what you must keep believing. The fairy-tale you have to keep telling yourself. Everybody now. After me. Bluebottles and butterfish, geckos and newts. Sidewinders. Willets. Pewits, terns, and

WHEN BARBARA WALTERS leans forward to emphasize her next question, Brandon Bazin seizes his chance and meets her with an open-mouthed kiss. They are floating in a hot fragrant bubble bath, submerged up to their shoulders. Brandon feels tingly and aware. He has never kissed an old lady before, except his mother and those weird aunts from Cedar Rapids. Barbara's body loosens in his arms. She reciprocates with her tongue. Her bony hand slides down between his legs through the water and squeezes. Brandon gets an instantaneous erection so hard it hurts. Chest swelling with optimism, he doesn't know what it is he has been looking for all his life, but he knows this is it. A single red rose leans in a green glass vase at the far end of the tub. Brandon reaches forward to offer it to Barbara, but by chance his elbow knocks into the boombox playing Plato's Deathmetal Tumors on the stool beside him. The boombox tips before either can respond and splashes into the sudsy water in a silverwhite flash of sparks and smoke. Barbara Walters and Brandon Bazin lunge and twist in place.

165

OH MY, WORRIES BETSI BLISS. Something is happening, but what? Nothing was happening and then something began happening. Then the next thing happened before Betsi had a chance to understand the last. And presently more things are happening one after the other after the other. Everything seemed so straightforward a minute ago. Now it's all sixes and sevens. Perhaps what is happening is a preview for one of those French films. If so, this is why Betsi Bliss prefers American food. Something continues to happen, and at the moment Betsi has no idea what is going to happen after it. She cannot put her finger on it, exactly, but she senses maybe she is becoming somehow more abstract. She doesn't quite know what she means by that, but she certainly does feel lost.

166

A SHRIEKING FROM ABOVE. Byron looks up from his deck of cards. He sees his buddies throwing themselves onto their stomachs, hands clamping down over helmets. His own body begins a slo-mo push forward to join them, but it is too late. The mortar slugs in.

167

"JESUS H. *CHRIST!*" Fred Quock's father shouts, throwing open the door to Leni's room with a bang. "Turn that goddamn noise duh--" He stops, arms flopping to his sides, face slackening as he takes in the view. "What ... what the hell's going on here? Freddy, you're wearing a dress. What in god's name is my son doing wearing a *dress?*"

"STOP IT!" MOIRA SCREAMS. "Please stop!" The big one with the smile that won't go away is slapping her around the mouth and cheeks with the back of his hand. She can taste blood and the taste scares her. She can smell a match igniting, then cigarette smoke. Blindfolded, Moira wafts in nighttime, waiting for what will happen next. The first burn hisses on her thighskin. She lunges and twists in place, but the strips of pillowcase holding her wrists and ankles to the bedposts are too tight. She can't make any progress. Her blindfold slips up a little on the left. She makes out the nervous second boy leaning against the wall, football helmet still beneath his arm, watching them all. The boy leisurely slides his free hand down the front of his pants. Another cigarette kiss. "Please!" Moira screams. "I can't remember my goddamn safety word! Cut it out! It *hurts!*" A set of heavy knuckles cracks into her right temple. Light swarms her head. Moira hopes the video camera on the tripod is able to capture her look of disbelief mixed with anguish.

169

"HEY, HEY, BABES," SAYS VLADISLAV, swaggering up to the two girls. His erection, wedged between the elastic of his black Calvin Klein briefs and his left leg, smarts. "Feel like a little company this afternoon?" The girls don't break eye contact with each other. "I'm not your type," says the one with the small gold ring at the corner of her mouth. "I'm not inflatable." "If I throw a stick," says the one with glazed-plum lipstick, "will you leave?" Then they continue their conversation as if Vladislav isn't there. He looks from one to the other expectantly, waiting for an opening, waiting for one of them to acknowledge the joke and invite him into it. He looks some more. And then, behind him, an explosion. Silverwhite glare. The rolling shockwave. The arcade a windstorm of shrapnel.

170

WHAT THE HELL JUST HAPPENED? Sid Münsterberg wonders, everything all at once black and dusty. He is lying on his side. His right shoulder is numb. He tries to remember what he saw just before the blast. That fat man hefting himself slowly out of his seat, candy boxes, popcorn tub, and cartons junked with food dropping away from him. How he rotated with difficulty to face the projection booth and how his arms rose up along his sides, launched out, spread wide, as if he were offering his chest to the lightmist bombarding him. Only then, his bloodstream lighting up with adrenalin, did Sid put together that something was out of the ordinary. He could make out a device in the guy's right hand. It looked like a joystick. Next he could feel his own body begin a slo-mo push forward over the empty seat in front of him, but it was too late. The fat man tilted back his head, closed his eyes, opened his mouth, and squeezed the trigger. *Stay calm*, Sid tells himself, pinned beneath smoking debris, a shrill squeal cycling in his ears. *It's okay. It's all right. This is exactly what the emergency response teams have trained for. Everybody's going to be fine, just fine. Hold on tight. It's beginning.*

ALL AT ONCE RYAN MOODY finds himself on his back beneath jagged rubble, baked dust singing his sinuses, the seat he was sitting in seconds ago somehow on top of him. He tries to get his bearings. It must be snowing through the wide gray absence above him. He can feel icy flakes kissing his thighskin through his shredded jeans. His ears feel clogged with water. He assumes he has gone deaf. Then, in stages, everything muffled, he begins to pick out the girl in front of him crying, and somebody nearby starting to moan. Other dazed voices lift here and there from the wreckage and, beyond, an alarm cycling deliriously.

172

THE GIRLS SCREAM. Vladislav shoves them to the grated metal floor, drops and rolls, freeing his Glock and opening fire. *"Stop it!"* they cry out behind him, covering their ears. *"Please stop!"* "Stay down!" he shouts back. It is hard to tell where he is in this existential dimness, how many there are out there, but they are well armed and just keep coming. He pegs one in the head, another in the upper chest, takes off another's kneecap. Momentum spins the last guy in a ski mask and night goggles through a flimsy banister, except he is somehow able to ignite an incendiary device as he goes over. What looks like a joystick twirls through the air in slo-mo, then *plups* into a vat filled with black liquid. Everything is flawlessly still. Then the blast. The girls wail. Vladislav ducks and covers. How in the world can he have an erection at a time like this? He closes his eyes, knowing he has to concentrate. The windstorm of shrapnel whirls into him.

173

TRAPPED BENEATH THE WRECKAGE, Garrett Keeter thinks it is cigarette smoke he smells. The tang quickly thickens and turns acidic. When the first burn hisses into his thighskin, he understands with a jolt the theater is on fire. He has traveled all these miles, covered all this geographical and psychic distance, and here he is, caught in a real-life disaster film. Close by, Jaci makes stunned whimpering sounds. Garrett tries to reach out to comfort her, only something is pinning down his arm. He tries to speak, only his jaw won't move. Flames lick his legs. Garrett Keeter cries out as he feels himself slipping beneath burning waves.

SOMEWHERE BELOW THE SOUL of Remedios the Beauty, a secondary explosion, then silverwhite light flocking toward her through the ventilation system. In the instant before it arrives with a fiery kiss, she remembers the day her great-grandfather, José Arcadio Segundo, having vanished for years into the jungle in search of a waterway connecting Macondo to the sea, unexpectedly floated into view on the river in a rickety steamboat filled with prostitutes. Since he did not succeed in finding the course he had been questing for, he decided to celebrate his failure instead. That evening he threw a Festival of Disappointment on the Street of Turks. Remedios the Beauty was crowned queen, not because of her looks (she had shaved her head with a dull razor that morning), but because of her wondrous cinnamon-and-orange scent. As the master of ceremonies lowered the rusty clothes hanger standing in for a coronet onto her head, a rival queen in a magnificent white lace dress and abundant veil came into sight at the far end of the block. An enormous entourage of nuns flooded around her. A wary hush swelled through the revelers. Even the prostitutes ceased laughing. One of the nuns shed her habit. In her place stood a soldier with a rifle.

175

He raised the weapon above his head, shouted something Remedios the Beauty could not comprehend, and the holy entourage turned quickly into an unholy platoon. With that, the Banana Company Massacre commenced. When a bullet took off José Arcadio Segundo's kneecap twenty-two inches to Remedios the Beauty's left, and her great-grandfather crumpled into a pile of useless old clothes beside her, Remedios the Beauty felt something tingle in the bottoms of her bare feet for the first time in her life, and realized her future would be nothing if not curious.

"HANG IN THERE, PEOPLE!" Josh Hartnett shouts,
scrabbling over chunks of fallen concrete, rebar,
upturned seats. "I'm Josh Hartnett, the actor! Help's
on the way!" His eyes sear. He has a hard time
catching his breath. But he scrabbles forward
searching for survivors. In his mind's eye, he is Staff
Sergeant Matt Eversmann in *Black Hawk Down* and
his mission is to boost his men's morale no matter   177
what. They are pinned down in the streets of
Mogadishu. They are taking heavy fire. It's up to
him to get them through alive. He closes his eyes,
knowing he has to concentrate. This is no time to
let his attention drift. This is no time to mess up a
good thing. Only he can't figure out why no one
has showed up to lend a hand yet. The exit doors
remain shut, the lobby silent. Where is everybody?
Emergency personnel should be thronging this place
by now. Josh can't figure it. Then he notices he is
holding something in his right hand. Knotty, bristly,
wet. He glances down. Through the dust and smoke,
he sees his soggy Irish tweed walking hat and fake
goatee. Something in him liquefies. Shit, man. Shit.
This isn't a stupid movie. He's no Army Ranger.
This is the real deal, and he's just Josh Hartnett, the
schmuck with really nice eyes. He drops his hat and

goatee. "Help us!" he screams. "Oh, god, help us! Help us! We're all gonna die! Stand by to crash! Help! *Help us!* HELP!"

FIRE CRACKLES. THE ALARM CYCLES. Susie Carbonara sobs quietly to herself beneath debris, waiting to die. She is thinking about how she lived a super life with Ronny and Tyler and Taylor, how she always tried as hard as she could to be a good Christian. She made mistakes. Everyone makes mistakes ... even if she can't quite call up any particulars at the moment. Isn't that funny? Nor can she fathom this is where it will end. After all the work she did for the homeless, all the daily greeting cards she posted to Our Maker. Hope, Susie decides, sobbing, is a joke. Everyone is trapped here. Everyone is doomed. This evening Sophia Choi on CNN will refer to what happened as *a terrible tragedy*. Susie finds it harder and harder to catch her breath. Her sole wish is that time will speed up now like in one of those movies, her world quickly become a what's that word jump-cut to the final credits. Close by, Juanita makes whimpering noises. Susie attempts reaching out her hand to comfort her, but touches something knotty, bristly, and round instead. She retracts to find a shrunken head gawking back at her from her open palm. Susie Carbonara shrieks in terror.

179

THE EXIT DOORS SMASH OPEN. They don't.
Firemen flood in. Ropes spaghetti down the edges
of the cavernous hole in the ceiling. S.W.A.T. teams
rappel, semi-automatic Heckler and Koch MP5's
blazing. The smoke. The dust. Or it is something
else. They do or they don't. One or the. Because in
the gray absence above, a copter leaps into view,
180 snow swirling in its downdraft. No, wait. That's
not right. The copter doesn't leap into view.
Everything is as it was. Everything is. What? A
Sunday afternoon at the movies. Then the fat man
slowly stands and slowly turns. He remains seated.
The audience watches. The exit doors. The firemen.
Is this another commercial? Anything's possible.
The S.W.A.T. teams rappel. But next. After that.
Subsequently. It's hard to say what. The second
bomb, the one under that man's mackintosh. A
firestorm whooshes out from him. Maybe. Maybe
not. Another section of roof. The Mall of America
is under attack. Yes, that's it. Other suicide bombers,
other floors. You can hear them. You can hear the
screams. The dynamics of metaphor. Chaos in the
atrium. And then: a ruptured waterpipe. Sections
of floor gape open. People, seats, chunks of concrete
disappear. A magic act. Use your. No. Imagination.

Wait. That's not right. How can you imagine such things? But afterwards, it's something else. It's one thing and then it's another. In the course of time. If you don't use it, somebody else will. And so. Next. Later on. As things worked out. It's the. What? Listen. Machinegun chatter. The rush of flames. The panicked shouts. The harsh cold wind blowing. Only that. None of it. All. Next the. And after that? What happens after that? And then what? What then?

MILO MAGNANI, one of the assistant managers of the Mall of America, loves watching trailers for disaster movies. But he loves watching his clients watch trailers for disaster movies even more. This is why two minutes ago he slipped unnoticed behind Byron Metnick during his, Milo's, afternoon walkabout and took the first seat in the very last row. From here, Milo can enjoy the view, not of the screen, but of the crowd sprinkled before him enjoying the view. Milo turns fifty-seven today. These next few minutes are a small birthday present to himself. Arms crossed above his generous belly, American-flag bowtie knotted beneath his chalky shaven wattle, Milo loosens his hold on his thoughts and finds himself back in Edina, Minnesota, site of Southdale, the first enclosed, multi-level mall in the United States. Milo's mother took him there for his eighth birthday in 1956, two months after its grand opening. Milo understood what he wanted to be when he grew up the second he walked through the entrance and saw the awesome sight of seventy-two stores stretching out ahead of him. It felt like a series of signposts to the future. Southdale was the creation of a man named Victor Gruen, an Austrian-born architect who, fleeing the Nazis, arrived in this country with eight bucks in his pocket and the belief that for communities to work well they needed to provide spaces for people to exist together. The advent of the automobile and suburbs had effectively blocked that possibility, so he invented a new kind of zone for human activity. People wouldn't only want to enter it to shop. They would want to enter it to *be*--stroll, sit, eat, chat, browse, play games, take simple pleasure in the rush of data and the presence of others--just like they used to do in the pedestrian arcades back in Europe. And look at where Victor's vision has led. You could fit seven Yankee stadiums into this place. *Seven.* Shortly after that visit, Milo came to understand something else about himself: that, if he relaxed just right, loosened his hold on his thoughts, he was sometimes able to slip behind the foreheads of those who had recently opened themselves up to the prospect of diversion-

a gift that has provided him with a consistent edge in his business. Right now, Milo is sliding into the cold hazy awareness of the old guy in the wheelchair at the far end of his row and apprehending that the sad, agitated ghost of his wife has just stopped by there for the last time, leaving behind a small residue of love, like a gold earring, before going away forever. The teenager in front of him is named Miguel Gonzalez, and Miguel Gonzalez is wondering why humans possess souls, if this is an example of what having one feels like. The girl beside him is feeling guilty Miguel paid so much money for a lousy afternoon with her. In row eleven, a cop named Sid Münsterberg scratches his burning toes through the scuffed-up leather of his cowboy boots, theorizing people go to movies because they feel they are actually buying the time to watch them. An unshaven young man in sunglasses touches his back pocket, all of a sudden aware his wallet is missing-- but that's all right, he figures, because he has made $27,987.53 on the New York Stock Exchange since entering here an hour ago. Vladislav Dovzhenko stealthily reaches up and cups his own left biceps as if cupping the breast of a teenage girl from San Diego. In row ten, an anorexic woman kisses Cary Grant through her surgical mask, and Cary Grant whispers gently into her ear that he prefers men, which she knows immediately is a lie. "We were just playing," Fred Quock tells his shocked father, "honest," to which his sister Leni adds hastily: "He made me do it, daddy. Freddy made me do it." Claude Méliès loves his wife almost undetectably more than he did four seconds earlier. Mouche sniffles beside him, her slight sinus cold having escalated into viral sloppiness, and thinks: *halcyon*. Vito Paluso assumes Mouche is sad, not sick, and feels sorry for the couple for the fight they just had. In row nine, Celan Solen resolves to drop in at Mona's apartment after the film because she told him she was going to be busy doing exactly nothing special all day. Next to him, Betsi Bliss experiences another slight dilation around her, reality a gleaming pulse, and reaches up to massage the flesh between her shoulder blades, anxious to see what her body's language has to say. Nadi Slone observes herself leaning uncomfortably against the window of a 747 thirty-eight thousand feet above a nighttime Atlantic, trying to sleep, and failing. Elmore Norman stands over his grill at Malaysian Madness, staring down at the veggies sautéing before him, mind blank as a burgled bank vault. Jerry Roemer leaps across his dewy backyard beneath a moonlit night like

Baryshnikov in *Swan Lake,* fifty years younger and wearing nothing but pink socks and blue sneakers. Betty Roemer sits by her phone at 4:42 a.m. in her room at the Adoring Care Retirement Home in Sarasota, Florida, lamenting there is no one left alive in her solar system to call. In row eight, Moira Lovelace looks forward to introducing biquadratic polynomial expressions to her junior math class tomorrow. Leon Mopati coughs discreetly into his palm and on the spot loses the train of thought he has been riding for several minutes. Giuseppe Rosi taps the send icon on his handheld and his threatening message to Stuart Navidson blinks into the electromagnetic fields around him. Thirty feet above, the mouse skittering through the warm darkness of the ventilation system stops dead in its tracks, sensing the presence of a cat somewhere below, then hurries on its infinite way. The cat, having already forgotten the pain in its side, wanders beneath Garrett Keeter's seat and eases onto its haunches, unaware as it licks its right paw that by crossing the highway in two hours and forty minutes it will force Garrett's car into a deadly skid. Garrett sees Jaci's and his silver BMW start gracefully and inexorably easing across the lanes into the sparkling lights of oncoming traffic, then jerks out of his doze, thinking: *stupid dreams.* Jaci smiles at nothing, catches herself, and stops. Ryan Moody the lesbian actor sits with a cold towel wrapped around her face in her dressing room in an alternate universe, crying lightly over her lover who just slammed the door behind her in a fit of hormonal pique. In row seven, Jeff Kotcheff crunches down on a handful of chips hard as he can, hoping to annoy the jewboy slumped in front of him. Josh Hartnett huffs to himself in unconditional anonymity and places slightly more weight on his left buttock than his right. Anderson Bates contemplates how, if you look across the Grand Canyon, you are really seeing the other side as it appeared about one ten-thousandth of a second earlier. In row six, Ida Jarboe devotes her full attention to a furuncular anomaly she has just discovered behind her left ear. Johnny Ray stands in the middle of a field of pot plants at night, waving at a bright triangle in the sky that grows smaller and smaller until it winks out of being, experiencing for the first time in his life what real loneliness feels like. Arnold Frankenheimer finds himself all at once unnerved, trying to remember whether or not he wiped that file of the college freshmen and the German shepherd from his hard drive before turning off his office lights and walking.

Stuart Navidson stops counting backwards. Kenneth Jehovah falls in love with Julia Ward Howe's astonishing intellect once again. Lying beside Christopher or Brian or David after making missionary love in the dark, Lara McLuhan says in her little girl's voice: *Tell me again, daddy. Tell it to me one more time.* In row five, Lewis Smoodin surreptitiously slaps himself stingingly across the face and in a flush of shame prays no one noticed. In row four, Lily Grodal catches herself wondering briefly how big her neighbor Anderson Bates's cock is, reddening in embarrassment, disbelief, and alert interest at the idea. Athena Fulay passes a stranger's blood back and forth over her tastebuds while a gentle affection inflates inside her for the man seated before her. Ed Bergman attempts to restrain himself from reaching forward and fingering the rubbery fabric of the black mackintosh twenty-two inches away. Susie Carbonara strolls through Camp Snoopy, reveling in the cotton-candy snowdrifts and wishing *she* could be that creative. Juanita Chamorro decides she will begin her long hike back home tomorrow morning. In row three, Kate Frazey is a limp puppet piled on the side of a dark road. Pierre searches his shirt pocket for his package of Juicy Fruit gum only to recall he left it in his other pair of khakis. Rex Wigglie decides his next lyric will involve both a falcon *and* a fish, then grins at his lyrical acumen. In row two, Lakeesha Johnson runs out of things to say to the no one on the other end of her cell phone and brings to a close the conversation that never took place. Chantrelle Williams's stomach burbles and she steals a glance over at Desria to see if she heard. Desria Brown stands with her hands in the pockets of her hooded sweatshirt, cold air leaking from her nose and mouth, watching a crumpled-up Starbucks coffee cup skip down the windy sidewalk in front of her, hop off the curb, and spin farther and farther up the vacant street. Milo Magnani glows with quiet pride, gives their thoughts back to these people, and, straightening his bowtie unnecessarily, rises to depart. Around him, throats clear, feet scrape, candy wrappers crinkle. The world grows brighter and brighter and brighter. Milo inhales and exhales. He waits. The film begins.

Printed in the United States
36144LVS00002B/79